My Vision – My Fiction
Series by
J. J. BALOCH

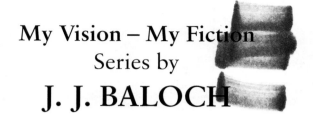

# Whiter
## than
# White

The Daughter of the Land of Pure

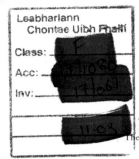
Matador
9 Priory Business Park,
Wistow Road, Kibworth Beauchamp,
Leicestershire. LE8 0RX
Tel: 0116 279 2299
Email: books@troubador.co.uk
Web: www.troubador.co.uk/matador
Twitter: @matadorbooks

ISBN 978 1788036 641

British Library Cataloguing in Publication Data.
A catalogue record for this book is available from the British Library.

Printed and bound by CPI Group (UK) Ltd, Croydon, CR0 4YY
Typeset in 11pt Adobe Garamond Pro by Troubador Publishing Ltd, Leicester, UK

Matador is an imprint of Troubador Publishing Ltd

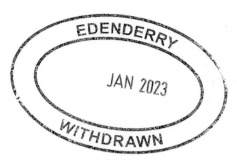

*Dedicated*
*To*
*Muhtarma Benazir Bhutto*
*Ex-Prime Minister*
*of*
*Pakistan*
*(Shaheed-Martyr)*
*&*
*Malala Yousafzai*
*Youngest female Education Advocate*
*for*
*Pakistani Women*

# Acknowledgement

Why I wrote this novel? What forced me to tell a story?

The credit goes to the police service of Pakistan which exposed society and its sensitivities to me. The truths so unearthed intrigued me to come with a voice that makes my fiction the way as *Whiter than White* brings out.

Besides my professional and personal exposure to gender vulnerabilities, what really prompted me to write a novel was the desire of my family to see me growing as a story teller; so I did accomplish this piece of fiction.

In this regard, first inspiration came from my daughter, Areesha Mehsheed. Areesha reads novels extensively and had perhaps smelled in my writings a hibernating story teller. She used to say: "Dad you have stuff and style; you have many stories to tell the world."

So, I started telling my first ever story in *Whiter than White: the daughter of the land of pure*. Besides this, my wife Faiza also kept on bucking me up all the time with accolades for my inspiring way as she takes it.

I also thank my son Muhammad Ali Ebraheem and my daughter Kiswah Kehaf who invoked in me my sleeping creativity by their innocent genius of telling me the stories of cartoons.

I am also highly thankful to my best buddy and a cop

colleague Irfan Ali Baloch, and my mentor Muhammad Ali Nekokara who stood by me in all odds in the process of inking this novel. I also extend my heartiest thanks to my friends and colleagues i.e. Omar Shahid Hamid (Himself Novelist) Nasir Aftab, Mr. Syed Pir Muhammad Shah, and Faisal Aziz khan (A Journalist) for their very inspirational words.

I am also grateful to Mr. Arshad Hussain Leghari and Mr Waseem Mughul for bearing with me as my facilitators in dealing with Matador staff emails and other issues.

I extend my special thanks to the editor of my novel Sophie Bristow and also proof reader Rachel Denton who did put their efforts to give fine and final finishing to its manuscript.

My special thanks to Rosie Lowe who marshalled the process of my novel's productions in a very cordial and congenial way.

I can take this opportunity to offer my profound thanks to Matador publications and their entire staff and all ranks who extended their timely, sincere, and all out support to me during the process of the production of this novel.

# About the Author

Javed Jiskani Baloch, author of *The Power of Social Media & Policing Challenges* and *On the Art of Writing Essays* is now coming up with his debut novel: *Whiter than White: The Daughter of the Land of Pure*. He writes in newspapers and magazines on issues of general interest with his focus on policing innovations, Human rights issues, governance, counterterrorism, counter-extremism, social media and radicalization of youth and also geostrategic vision in South Asia. Academically, J. J. Baloch has done triple masters. He is MSc Criminal Justice Policy from London School of Economics & Political Science, London UK. He also did his MA Sociology as well as MA International Relations from University of Sindh Jamshoro.

Professionally, after serving as a bank officer for five years, J.J. Baloch joined prestigious civil services of Pakistan after qualifying competitive exam for Central Superior Services (CSS). Now he is a senior police officer with a reputation of being a fearless cop, incredible crime-fighter and a hard-task master. His exemplary works in policing have earned him a large fan following in Pakistan and abroad. J.J. Baloch has grown as a cherished cop among his junior officers and youngsters who yearn to become police officers and writers.

# Chapter One

It was a dreadfully dark night. It had rained cats and dogs shortly before. Alan's house was in deep jungle in the arms of the Indus River. The trails in the area were flooded and were denying anything an access to blaze them. Voices of creatures of the night were vibrant and punchy in otherwise immune from human sounds environs, except the awful roar of the fast-flowing river. The sky wore a sheet of dark clouds. Misfortune was hovering over Alan's house.

Alan had a wife named Sadori (meaning Lucky) and a baby girl named Janat (Paradise) of only eight months old. Sadori had a habit of speaking while asleep. That rainy night's voices and sounds disturbed Alan's sleep. He was lying on the bed with his wife but his mind was awake.

A storm was brewing. Alan's wife began her sleep talk. First, she moved her body and tried to detach herself from someone who seemed to be trying to hold her fast. She was moving her arms and her bangles were releasing irritating sounds, getting on Alan's nerves. She, in her struggle to get away from someone, spoke and Alan heard her saying: 'Sakhie (meaning benevolent man) leave my hand, I am married and have a kid, and so it is not possible for me to continue having extramarital relations with you. Please forget what happened and forgive me for my limits." She, perhaps, dropped a bombshell on Alan by uttering these words.

Though a bolt from the blue, yet the content of the sleep talk by his wife blew Alan's top like anything. Being up in arms and having his hands on his head, Alan decided to skin his wife alive. Anger and rage blinded Alan; his eyes were rolling and he was breathing fast. He was quite out of mind and heart for any sympathy for Sadori who, Alan was thinking, had stabbed in his back.

Alan was going mindless and ballistic. He began questioning himself as to why he lived to see such a humiliation and dishonour as he had understood the scenario. Between these two options, Alan was to go for one. As per his inner judge, Alan did not see himself worthy of dying for a woman who had allegedly betrayed him, so the only option left for him was to kill his wife. The disturbing factor was his eight-month-old girl, Janat. The devil was on full-time duty playing with the feelings of Alan who reached the point of strong doubt that his blood was running in the body of his daughter and that she was the illegitimate daughter of Sakhie. Therefore, in Alan's scheme of things, little doll, Janat deserved to die.

So, Alan went into kitchen, found a knife and came back to the room with the knife in his hand. His wife was awake by then. She was busy feeding her infant daughter. The ruthless husband stabbed his wife to death. Janat fell down from her hands onto the floor. The room was cluttered with bloodstains. The infant was crying in hunger and pain; while her mother Sadori was lying on the bed, counting her last breaths. The callous Alan took his little 'paradise' to throw her into the flowing river alive and he did it in a very cold-blooded way. This hair-raising event was not much remembered because hardly anyone came to know except close family members of

Alan who were not satisfied even with his brutality but wanted still more inhuman action. Staggeringly, no one in Alan's family was worried about his worst-of-its-kind act; rather they pampered and patted Alan for having saved their so-called family honour.

Alan succeeded in hushing up the matter. He bribed local police and mollified his in-laws on the grounds that his wife Sadori had brought bad name to his family and he had killed her to defend his family honour.

Alan went scot-free: he and his in-laws kept the double murder of Sadori and his daughter Janat in cold storage. No complaint was made to police nor was this incident reported. The secret news of this unfortunate incident travelled but only in between the family ears of Alan and his in-laws who had already gone very defensive on account of their daughter's alleged relations with Sakhie. Police neither heard any whistle-blowing from any corner about the murder incident, nor could find any plausible evidence in the absence of a private complainant. Rather the police made an underhand deal with Alan for keeping silent. As a result, there was no smoking gun to implicate Alan in a double murder crime. This whole episode was, indeed, very flabbergasting.

However, after two years a private and parallel justice system called Jirga came into action on the complaint of Alan. Alan's family took the poor man Sakhie to task for his being allegedly a reason behind the double murder of mother, Sadori and daughter, Janat at the hands of Alan. As a result, Sakhie agreed to enter into a tribal dialogue and had made up his mind to pay damages, if so proved, to wash his sins and to save his life from the vengeance of Alan and his family. A *Jirga* a private jury of tribal notables for settling tribal, property and honour disputes is believed to be an expeditious and an inexpensive process of redressal of grievances and burying hatchets among people in many parts of rural areas in Pakistan and Afghanistan.

# Chapter Two

*Three years later…*

Three years after the double murder was committed by Alan, a local private jury of tribal chiefs called *Jirga*, with the assistance of some notables, took place at Kashmor district and city Kashmor Sindh. This must catch our interest in that, in such private trial, the actual murderer, Alan, was not being tried but rather he was the complainant.

His complaint was against the accused, Sakhie, who was blamed for having had extramarital terms with the slain wife of Alan, Sadori. Alan had killed Sadori and her daughter of eight months, Janat, in a bid to save his family honour as per his claims and complaint.

The *Jirga* system in our part of the world is a sort of a parallel justice system in its essence but in its form, *Jirgas* run counter to what we understand as a parallel justice system as they are understood in American and European settings. In settings of the civilized world, such systems of *Jirgas* can be described as the 'anti-rule of law injustice systems', which derive their justifications from cultural traditions of the regions of their practice and acceptance.

In the civilized world the private justice system grows on moral justifications of supporting and building a victim's life but here in our sub-continental set-ups, this system of *Jirgas* survives on protecting and building the lives of real culprits and destroying the lives of the innocents who are not even yet born in this world. To anybody's extreme horror, the miscarriage of justice, so resulting, awaits the birth of the victims. It looks quite strange to many people reading this script but as a matter of fact it is a social reality for us to co-exist with.

*Jirga* courts function with communal and tribal rules and ethics; they know no laws. Both the community of the complainant as well as the accused form such private juries with the consensus to resolve disputes resulting out of honour disputes such as the one in point here. If either of both communities in dispute does not do this or fails to comply with the decisions of *Jirga*, a killing spree ensues unabated, leaving many families homeless, many children orphaned, many women widows, many mothers issueless or childless, and many people from both sides of the disputing and conflicting tribes going bankrupt and in some cases becoming homeless beggars. The law of the jungle reigns supreme in such situations.

After the killing of Sadori and Janat by Alan, the father, mother and brothers of his slain wife did not condemn and castigate Alan for having killed his innocent wife and daughter but rather they went ahead in motivating Alan to kill Sakhie to complete the justice as, according to them, their girl was killed by her husband under allegation of having suspected extramarital relations with a man who as per traditions should have been awarded the same punishment of murder. They stood with Alan to get *Jirga* compensation from the accused and to wage a war against the opponent tribe. In such wars what has been the main practice against those who deny *Jirga* is the kidnapping of the opponent-tribe's females and making forced marriages with them. In such cases sometimes even married women fall victims to the beasts who kidnap them, keep them at gunpoint until their terms are negotiated in *Jirga*. Fearing all this, Sakhie got his tribe involved in negotiating and finding a solution ever since the day he was accused and Sadori was killed. Though Sakhie claimed to have had no extramarital relations with Sadori, yet he had liked her before her marriage and he never saw her after she was wedded, as he stated.

How this all happened in the twenty-first century is what Sakhie's unfair trial revealed with alarming clarity! It was Sunday. Both tribes had come face-to-face at the address of a local tribal notable to negotiate the deal of double murder. One *Ameen* (Chief Judge/reconciliator) of *Jirga* conducted himself as the final authority, who announced the judgement, who was nominated with the consensus of both tribes and who was preferably a third party, not belonging to either of the disputing tribes. The tribes in dispute were represented by their respective tribal negotiators called 'salis', who acted as advocates for the tribes they belonged to. The womenfolk of the warring tribes were kept uninformed about what was going on in *Jirga* proceedings.

In this historic *Jirga* (jury) of the trial of innocents, the tribal bench constituted Samandar Khan (name meaning 'head of seas') as chief justice or *Ameen* meaning 'protector of peace', Darya Khan (name meaning 'head of rivers') and Jungle Khan (name meaning 'head of jungle') both as salis of their respective tribes. About fifty people from each tribe joined the jury proceedings. Proceedings began at 10am on, a Sunday in a government-owned rest-house of the irrigation department, right on the banks of the River Indus in Kashmor town, in the district of Kandhkot in Sindh.

First, Jungle Khan, representing the Alan party, started

reading the written charge sheet or statement of allegations against Sakhie. The charge sheet is reproduced here:

'Mr. Sakhie son of Nawab Khan is charged with violation of our family honour by having been involved in an illicit relationship with a married woman, the late Mrs Sadori wife of Alan. Alan killed his wife on strong suspicion that his wife, Sadori, had illicit relations with Mr. Sakhie. Alan also had serious suspicions that his daughter Janat was the illegitimate daughter of Sakhie. Alan produced the evidence of his wife's talking in her sleep as her confession. Since there was no eyewitness who had seen Alan killing his wife and his daughter except his honest confession, there appeared no other valid reason for their being killed except strong doubt emanating from human emotions and feelings of betrayal. Having killed his wife and daughter as a matter of honour, Alan has left us with no doubt that the accused was involved in what Alan argued. We need an explanation from Sakhie as to why penalty as per our indigenous customs and traditions should not be imposed on him.'

On reading this statement, Jungle Khan informed the *Ameen* or head of Jirga that he was ready to reply to any query on the part of the tribe he was representing. *Ameen* of *Jirga* agreed. Jungle sat and Darya Khan a *salis* or advocate of Sakhie's party stood and sought permission to read his statement of defence while the rest of the participants observed great discipline and pin-drop silence while the proceedings were going on. The head of Jirga granted permission to Darya Khan representing the accused party to read his statement of defence, which was as follows:

'I am representing the accused, Mr. Sakhie, who, to my information and knowledge, is innocent. We deny the allegations. We have had no illicit relations with any females. The allegations have no basis and no evidence; they are rather based on pure assumptions. In dreams and in realities things vary. Alan did not see Sakhie son of Nawaz Khan with his wife, nor yet has Alan proved any link of suspected relations with the infant girl who was killed by Alan for no sin at all. Doubt alone is not enough evidence to take someone's life that is very dear to someone. The innocence of the little girl, Janat, killed by her own father, speaks volumes about who is guilty and why. Alan is the killer of his wife and daughter, not Sakhie. Sadori and her daughter Janat were killed innocent. She should have been alive to speak out her mind. I deny Alan's allegation of Sakhie's involvement directly or indirectly in this matter. Therefore, I request the chief of Jirga to do justice to Sakhie. Had Alan been able to catch his wife red-handed with Sakhie, we community members would have stayed with him but the case is the other way round.'

After recording statements of both sides and hearing Alan and Sakhie with so many cross examination, the Jirga come out with the following decision:

'We have heard both the parties in all possible details. Complainant Alan maintained that his wife and his daughter lost their lives because of Sakhie and he is the main reason behind their beheading and throwing into water so he must be penalized severely for all this. While on the contrary, Sakhie and his supporters deny allegations and maintain that Sakhie is innocent. This party says the killer of both mother and daughter is Alan who confesses his guilt. Instead of trying Alan, Sakhie has been taken to task, which is unfair.

Keeping in view both points of view, this Jirga finds Sakhie guilty, as he admitted that before her marriage Sakhie had an emotional attachment with Sadori. Mr. Sakhie fails to plead innocent as Alan has killed his wife and infant daughter for which 'no other plausible reason' is traceable so the burden of proof is on Sakhie who has not been fully successful in convincing this Jirga about his 'complete innocence'. Therefore, in order to resolve this dispute once and for all, this Jirga fines Sakhie to pay Pakistan rupees of five lakhs to Alan as compensation on the one hand and a girl of Sakhie's family may be wedded to a male of Alan's family. This could iron out the differences between the two tribes, which, if left unattended, could progress into a big disaster. If Sakhie has no unmarried girl available in his family, he can promise in writing with this Jirga (jury) that whenever any girl is born in Sakhie's family, he will surely get her married to a boy from the family of Alan.'

Sakhie agreed and had no other option. Sakhie's tribe paid a cheque of 0.5 million rupees to Alan. Sakhie was issueless. However, after two years, Sakhie was blessed with a daughter who was wedded at the age of ten with the brother of Alan, named Waqar, a twenty-eight-year old young man. That unfortunate girl was none else but myself – Hoor. The background of my marriage at an early age was disclosed to me by my husband, Waqar, on my wedding night.

Waqar, my husband, narrated me this background of our marriage on our first wedding night, which was the most haunting night ever in my life. The memories of this background and wedding night have remained a grave scratch on my conscience, making me think, why was I such an unfortunate girl? Why did all this happen to me? My in-laws remained swayed in the feeling of unending grudge against me as an enemy bride. I have seen their intimidation tactics blurring their humanity. The tutting, heart-sinking, head-shaking and sneering comments of my mother-in-law kept following me round every corner of my life, until I succeeded in burying my woeful past.

# Chapter Three

I am a human being. I eat. I drink. I sleep. I think. I believe. I feel. I wish. I love as well as I hate. I am both the emotional and the rational entity as well. I understand what is wrong and what is right. I also communicate sense. I can do everything that is humanly possible. I am a woman. But, still, I am not a man, despite the fact that I have almost all that the man has! I have even more.

However, my culture is yet to treat me the way that it should or, in a more appropriate way, it is yet to take me as seriously as it takes a man.

I am a woman. I am not a man. I am not born with a silver spoon in my mouth. My society offers me scarce opportunities. My fight with my own destiny may be essentially similar to that of any other woman in the world, but I am damn sure there will be a negligible minority of females who have gone through the ordeals of life that I have. Both conditions in which I have been and the opportunities I have had are really very telling and very revealing in terms of highlighting the gravity as well as the magnitude of my war against the circumstances of what I am!

I am unlettered and I don't know what is going on only a mile away from my home. I feel I have been born not to know anything, not to use anything, not to own anything, not to talk for anything and also not to feel, think, or desire anything. My name is Hoor, meaning 'beautiful' in the local language. It applies not only to nomenclature; but, as my mirror tells me when I stand in front of it, I am damn beautiful and bewitching too.

The eyes of the sun, the touch of running water and of air thick with dust, cruelties of climate, tortures of time, severity of social taboos, lethargy of law, callousness of culture, sensitivities of state, disowning by parents, and bad intentions of the man always keep me in a state of utter retreat and utter helplessness despite the fact that I am a daughter, a sister, a wife and a mother.

I am lily-white because I have done nothing wrong in my life. My life has taught me lessons of 'giving' only. I get nothing in return. What gives me strength is my inner satisfaction that I can give something to somebody. I am not at least a burden on anybody.

I live in a forsaken place called Karachi Kacha, an island-type piece of land surrounded by Indus River water, falling in the administrative jurisdiction of district Rahim Yar Khan Punjab, the meeting point of borders and cultures of three provinces, Sindh, Balochistan, and Punjab. Let me take you to my area so that you may be able to follow what I want to say.

A *kacha* (unsettled) area is one that falls between the river (Indus in my case) and its protective embankments to protect communities living in settled (*Paka*) areas from floods. We live in a *kacha* or unsettled area. We remain always vulnerable to the horrors of water. There are thick jungles here. Populations are scattered and have separate, disposable homes of wood that they can dismantle and run away with, using donkeys as their mode of transport, in case of emergency. There is no electricity, no roads, no schools, no hospitals, no gyms, no pools, no five stars, no streets, no addresses, no telephones, no government, no law, and no TV.

But we do have a life here. We do have radios; we do have mobile phones, which we charge on batteries; and some amongst us do have lethal weapons. We hear about everything on these two battery-operated instruments.

Besides this, we have one thing you may be jealous of and that is 'pure nature' at its best with the minimum of carbo-techno impurities of modern life. And we do have our criminals and cattle as our economy.

The way of life and source of income of many families is crime as their profession, and weapons as their tools of labour. These people do not think that kidnapping and killing are bad acts.

Once I had a very serious dialogue with my father-in-law, Mr Rahim Bux, a seventy-six-year-old man who was very frank with me in talking about the wisdom behind their lifestyles. I expressed my concerns about why every other man in our area was holding *Hathyar* (weapon). I asked him, 'Why does everybody, even kids, hold *Hathyar*, instead of books and pens?'

On this question he gave me a very simple but astonishing answer in these words: 'Survival is important. If you tell any animal here to hold any book or pen, would he/she ever do that? I think never. What do they look for in satiating their hunger: books or food? Definitely food! We are human animals and we need to have food to survive.'

He further brought out:

'Lands here do not belong to us; they belong to feudals and people in high places politically. Government lands also belong to them. We depend on them. For our food and livelihood, we look forward to them and they, in turn, require us to keep weapons to protect their possessions here; but for buying weapons, we don't have money so we keep committing crime to earn money for food and weapons which help us survive poverty in a feudal society.'

'Uncle, but this is wrong way to terrorize innocent people,' I further commented.

He remarked on the point of terrorizing innocents, 'The wrong and right are two sides of the coin; what is wrong for you may be right for me and what seems to you wrong today may appear right tomorrow! So, this is a big debate of life but our stomach silences only with food not with logic of wrong and right. We are not the people with any capacity or power to frame the moral values of the system but we learn the norms of survival on our own. And this is what we do and this is how we live.'

I further asked him for my own clarity, 'But why are there weapons and why is there violence?'

He very politely told me, 'Yes, why weapons? It is a good question. We call weapons *Hathyar* in our language. *Hathyar* is a combination of two words: *hath* means 'hand' and *yar* means 'friend'. So *Hathyar* means 'friend of the hand'. But, remember, it is the friend of a hand that holds it. When we hold them we feel powerful and satisfy our inner person that we are not helpless and powerless. We make stories of bravery and gallantry only because of these weapons.'

'Uncle, your depiction makes me feel that nuisance and power convinces people to go armed rather than to suffer poverty and hunger,' I argued.

He further unveiled, 'We are the most disadvantaged people on earth. No one bothers how we live! How do our children grow up? Lands here belong either to government or to feudal lords, who are the real government and who use us as tissue paper. We neither have good memories of our forefathers, nor do we see any hope for our future generations to make some success in life. Kidnapping for ransom, extortion and target killing is our profession. Our men believe that being killed by law enforcement agencies is an honour for us.' My father-in-law further stated, 'if they (feudals) don't own us when we are alive, at least they can claim some reward price from the government when we are killed or dead.'

I learnt a lot but never got satisfied with the explanation of uncle, Rahim Bux. Being a woman, I lived in the crossfire. We neither fought with anybody nor got involved in any crime except that we were tied with our males in the promises of living and dying together which were something we were really helpless about. It was more tantalizing for us that our kids were growing in unhealthy and entirely hostile environment. On the one hand were the criminals whose non-compliance meant death while on the other hand were the cops who were to kill our kids if our kids comply with criminals or commit any crime. Our children grew up in constant fear of being killed. So with the passage of time, they cherished killing and wished to be killed rather than die of a heart attack or any other stupid reason. They felt pride being killed fighting their enemies who may be anyone fighting with our men for any good reason. Dying with a bullet was a source of great honour, so it was the fashion there that mothers prayed for and felt proud of their boys being killed by a bullet injury, while fighting their enemy.

# Chapter Four

It was Saturday night in the first week of December a gang of armed outlaws came to our home and called my husband, Waqar. I and my daughter, Zuhra, who was six and my son, Mehar, who was eight years old, got a whiff of something going wrong. It was windy outside. The river was getting drier. And there was a chilling cold all around. We were comfortable inside our room due to a wood fire, which we used to keep ourselves warm. I was between the devil and the deep blue sea as to what would happen with my hubby and I started praying to God for help and mercy.

My anxiety was because it was very well known in our area that these gangs tortured and killed if anybody gainsays them anything. There were also stories circulating that these notorious criminals had killed the whole family of a person who disallowed them access to his home due to his wife and daughters who he feared to be molested by those freaks. At times I started shivering. My ears were fixed in the direction of the compound wall trying to listen to what was going on. Suddenly I heard uproar. The gangsters were forcing my hubby to keep custody of a kidnapped man whom they were holding hostage, demanding a handsome amount for his release.

My husband got into a hot argument with them and explained to them his limits. His logic fell on deaf ears. They ultimately warned him to keep the unfortunate guy or go with them. My husband knew that if he left, there was no one left behind to protect his family from both hostile nature and inimical society. The demand they made was to arrange dinner for fifteen armed persons forthwith as, according to them, they had had empty stomachs for two days. My husband came with a half-yellow and half-red face, quite dithery and edgy. Ill at ease, Waqar ordered me to make dinner for them.

I understood his mixed expression of anger and depression, and hurriedly did everything. I cooked up a meal. He fed them. They delivered custody of the kidnapped man who was said to be a businessman from the Rahim Yar Khan district. They left us early in the morning. After that they remained in contact with my husband to enquire about the person. I made every possible effort knowing full well that the person in our custody must be a son, a father, a brother of so many people who must be waiting and crying for his safe return. And he told us he had four kids, a wife and an old mother who would die if he did not go back home safely.

My eyes went watery and I started crying when he told me that his younger son cannot sleep without him. His mother and his wife wait for him before eating dinner. He was not worried about how he was and where he was, but the thought of his family's wellbeing had haunted him like anything.

He asked me a favour: to make a call to his wife so that they may rest assured that he was alive. I was not in a position to do this due to the consequences that I was imagining would happen if something went wrong with the assignment of gangsters here.

One day, he was very tense and refused to take lunch. Waqar had gone to buy some food for us. He said: 'Sister, please help me; I am not running. I will stay here until I pay money to gangsters. Please, I want to hear the voice of my family.'

My heart went soft and I resolved to help him go back to his family as early as possible. Being a female and a mother, it was a very hard task for me. I gave him my phone to make a call to his wife on promise of not telling any police or any gangster.

I gave him my phone. I trusted him for not getting me in trouble. But, I ran a great risk for myself by so doing. He spoke to his family but in a language I was not able to understand but I saw he was crying and weeping. I knew full well that he did not know where he was right at that moment. So I felt a bit more secure that he couldn't help himself out. Waqar came and I did not tell him anything about the phone call.

To my utter surprise, early the next morning, police contingents raided our place. When Waqar saw police approaching, he stared at me with suspicion but as he was not sure exactly what had happened, he took his gun and got in position at his fence, to give the police a tough resistance.

Meanwhile, Waqar made a call to the gangster who had brought the kidnapped man to our home. I tried to convince Waqar not to put up resistance against the men in uniform because that could be disastrous but Waqar said: 'if I do not do it the ringleader of the gang will definitely kill me.'

Fighting with the police gave him a chance to survive but betraying a gangster was to invite death for his whole family. So he chose to take arms against the police as a Hobson's choice. Waqar had one G3 and 800 rounds. He had capacity to fight all day long. Waqar told me to hide myself and my kids behind big grave-like fences, which we had dug for protection. I did it.

When the police got closer Waqar fired straight at the advancing party and killed six policemen on the spot. The crossfire was getting intense. Waqar had strong nerves but my kids were in my lap and the kidnapped man was right next to us. I told him, 'If the police kill my husband I will kill you because we have reached this situation because of you even though we did not kidnap you.'

The captive was shivering. He was regretting. He was repenting. He had not thought this could happen. His wrong decision and breach of trust led us to that war which we had neither chosen nor prepared for.

After two hours of very intense fire from both sides, the gangsters made their very violent entry into the scene and took away the kidnapped man by killing three more police officers with one gangster suffering a slight injury. Waqar was left with two more criminals to fight with force. The ring leader was very selfish.

What he was concerned for was the safety of the kidnapped man because he wanted to get money for his return. That night Waqar had bought me new clothes. He told me to wear them for him. I did. I was looking pretty. When the jaundiced eye of the gangster, Meeral, fell on me, I felt embarrassed and became frozen for few moments. I had read his motives on his face. My conscience was pricking me. But I was helpless. I was worried for my family.

During this, I crawled to Waqar and told him that today the gangster will kill you. He told me I was stupid. He further said we had helped him; we had not betrayed him, so why would he kill him? I was not able to convince him for what I was suspecting as his time was counted.

After a little while the gangster told Waqar that he was

leaving his men with him to fight and engage the police, meanwhile he asked Waqar to send me and my kids with them to a safe place. I refused to go. Waqar was also insisting that I leave. Consequently, Meeral took our kids with the kidnapped man because he knew that my kids would drag me in their footsteps to his place.

Next day, gang men advised Waqar to leave his hearth and home for safety. Reportedly, police contingents had planned to raid that place. These criminals had nefarious designs of eliminating Waqar. Waqar and I left with gang men. The gunmen were loyal to their ringleader, Meeral. When we got into the boat to cross the River Indus, a sudden sniper shot hit Waqar right at his head and he fell straight into the river. I cried and wanted to follow him into the river but the gunmen controlled me and forcibly held me on the boat, taking their positions behind sandbags, which they were using as a shield.

I, perhaps, went into senselessness until we reportedly reached the *kacha* area of Sindh district, Ghotki, where Meeral was based and had a camp. My kids were not there. I kept on crying and asking Meeral why he had wronged me. I had lost everything. I lost my husband, my kids, my family, my home and my respect. I had lost even myself.

While consoling me, Meeral told me to forget everything. He tried to revive, saying that I was born anew. I told him that he had gone crazy. How could I forget my home, the time I spent with my husband, and how could I forget my sweet kids who might be hungry? How could I survive without my little princess Zuhra – my daughter – and my son, Mehar, who might be orphaned, helpless and crying for their parents? I promised Meeral: 'You are going to get nothing out of me. I am a dead body. I need to be reunited with my kids.' He urged,

'Marry me. Where would you go with two kids? Waqar was a good and brave fighter and my friend, so it is my responsibility to take care of you and your kids in all respects.' I lashed out at him, 'What are you talking about? I am ruined by a vicious circle of your own script! I have lost my husband, my family and myself. How do you expect me to marry you?'

He reacted in his criminal style, 'If you won't marry me, I will not let you marry anybody ever and will keep you here with me as my possession.' This annoyed me like anything, 'To hell with marriage; to hell with you; Keep my dead body you will never find me with you, and I unveiled to him. In me you will find an emotionless entity. He claimed to have fallen in love with me, arguing that both in love and war foul works well.'

He promised to bring back my kids to me. I wept the whole night and he put me with his existing two wives who revealed to me their horrifying and hair-raising tales of torture and agony. Both of them wept with me and advised me to comply with what he was demanding, failing which he would not stop harming me. But this state of utter anxiety would be all over once I got into a relationship with him. I had no way out but to go with the wind and I did. He forcibly got wedded with me within three months of my arrival there.

# Chapter Five

The place I came to was a little bit harder than the one I was living in earlier in Rahim Yar Khan Punjab. This was Ghotki Sindh district. Meeral's camp was in thick jungle, on an island, surrounded by water on all four sides and *Nag Wah* (Snake River) on its start. Perhaps, being a criminal, Meeral thought it quite a safe place for his hiding as he was carrying two million cash reward on his head, dead or alive! He was a notorious outlaw who was involved in a number of kidnappings and killings of both natives as well as foreigners, including police officers.

While living at this forsaken place, we had to face a number of difficulties for our livelihood. There were no shops, no marts, no shopping bazaars, but only raw and hostile nature, where we used to grow some vegetables and some cattle for milk and meat. We, as housewives, were responsible for cooking food for all people gathered at the camp of the chief outlaw who unfortunately happened to be the husband of all three females under shelter at his camp.

While doing the daily work of collecting sticks for lighting fires to cooking food and cutting grass for cattle, the questions always touched my mind: 'Is this the work we are born for? Are we females just the cheapest labour force or merely a childbearing machine that can give birth preferably to a baby boy? While on the contrary, if it happens to be a baby girl, why is the mother considered the most unfortunate one and a very bad omen for the honour and prosperity of the family? Hence, the mother is looked down upon solely for being the mother of a baby girl. What the males need is a male, a successor, their owner (*Waris*) and the owner of everything they have – their property, their honour, their name, their fame or notoriety, even their lives. A baby boy is deemed a symbol of luck, an avenger, a guardian of revenge and scores and a torch-bearer of bravery and masculinity.'

The part of the world I was living in and had lived in was male-dominated in its literal sense. It was a place where male cattle were valued higher than females. This was so because even in tribal feuds, which took place every year, women were discriminated by the feudals.

Very recently my cousin, named Skeena, had been killed on the pretext that an enemy tribe had attacked, killing one woman and her daughter of eight years. Whereas no enemy reportedly made any attack. It was Skeena's own in-laws, who killed her and her small daughter because they considered Skeena as a bringer of bad luck to that family due to her having given birth to a small baby girl. So when Skeena's in-laws killed two persons of another tribe over a dispute about land, the opposite party got the case registered against them at the police station of the area. Skeena's in-laws, in order to strike a compromise deal with the opponents and enemy tribe, wanted to implicate them in a fake counter-case with the intention of building pressure on them for withdrawing from the double murder case against the in-laws of Skeena.

Therefore, Sakina's in laws killed Skeena and her little daughter, thereby concocting the story that the enemy had attacked and killed two persons of their family only for getting a counter criminal case to be registered against the opponents so that they may come under extreme pressure and settle their land issue and withdraw the criminal cases against Skeena's in-laws which otherwise was a distant dream for them to realize.

I came to know the secrets because Skeena's in-laws sought the help of the chief outlaw, the person I had been wedded to very recently. He told me the story. My mom also confirmed to me about the drama of the murder of two innocent females. But these two unfortunate souls were brutally victimized due to the animalistic wishes of their males just for nothing, no sin, no wrong-doing, no crime, and no violation of any kind. Neither moral values nor family honour nor yet any law of the land, no promise, no commitment, no word at all was violated. But both were killed for nothing, just for no reason at all except the nefarious designs of their males to make them scapegoats.

The very heart-wrenching fact was that they were both killed by their own nearest and dearest ones for no reason and if they would have asked, if given a chance, I am damn sure they would have willingly sacrificed themselves for their husbands or for their fathers or for their brothers but they were not given that choice. So they were not only deprived of the choice of giving sacrifice for their family and finding some spiritual solace in it but also from their rights to life.

Having this state of agony in mind, I deduced: 'Dying with choice is better than being deprived of life unnoticed and without cause. Thus, this is not the only case but this is what I know and I have seen happening before us but there are hundreds and thousands of such stories of my people.'

The incident of the double murder made me very sceptical and insecure about myself and about my sweet princess,

Zuhra. One night I saw in a dream that Meeral was killing my daughter on the allegation that she could bring a bad name to his family honour and so he was arguing with me to get rid of my daughter. In the dream I cried like anything and tried to eschew the killing incident assuring Meeral and promising him that, 'I will kill my daughter with my own hands if I find her bringing a bad name to our family name or honour.'

So, I further requested him not to think badly about me and my daughter. He spared her with the words that he would kill us both, if he finds either of us, mother or daughter, violating the moral codes of family honour by establishing any kind of extramarital or love relation with any man. I woke up in an awful state. My heartbeat was pounding my eardrums like anything as if I had just been resuscitated from the grave.

I was under constant mental stress of falling victim to the doubts of this scoundrel who was without ideas, without mind, without reason but an adroit criminal, with high instinctive finesse, who used to believe, 'The man should not ignore four things in his life. First, he should eat whatever is available and should not wait for better food because you never know whether you could get it again or not. Secondly, when you find a reasonable place having dense shade from a tree do not forget to take rest and sleep because in jungles you never know whether you could find a better place or a better time for it. Thirdly, when you fight your enemy, never count how many you kill, just keep on killing because it is never sure when you could find such an opportunity again to create terror and awe which pays you and glorifies your name. Lastly, however sanguine your enemy is or may be, never kill their women but kill their men to take custody of women for loving them and for making those wives.'

Though I was in a marital relationship with that despicable meanie and baddie, yet my mind never accepted him nor yet was my heart ever at peace with him. I had my independent signature of ideas and emotions, lethally unmatched with most of the men, especially brutes like Meeral. I was to live with him because I was not left with any other option right at that moment. That was perhaps the only option available for me to bulwark my children. At the same time, I had no vehement vengeance against Meeral. I remained quiet and calm during three to five years of my marital relationship and I did not bear any baby for reasons I really have not been able to comprehend except that God did not will it. As Meeral had many kids both boys and girls from other two wives, he never bothered me to conceive a child. Nor did I ever wish one from him.

One day, I was washing family clothes on the bank of the River Indus. The riverine scene of water flowing surrounded by trees and grass was presenting a very snappy show of natural beauty. Suddenly, I saw a one-armed person approaching me. I became a bit nervous and uneasy, trying to cover myself so that he may not see me. When he reached five feet away from me, I asked him to stop there as my daughter was also with me.

He said: 'Sister, don't worry, please. I am not a bad guy, although a stranger, but if you are Hoor then I need to tell you one important thing.'

I was a little ambivalent and also confused as to how he knew me. But curiously, I replied, 'Yes, I am the one you are asking for!'

At this he said, 'I have come from Rahim Yar Khan to join Meeral's gang and I know Waqar who, too, was an outlaw and the ex-husband of the woman I am conversing with right at that moment.'

He further unveiled, 'Meeral first trapped Waqar and then conspired to kill him just to marry you; Waqar was not killed by Police fire. This is what everyone in gang circles knows.'

Hearing this startling news, the Earth just stopped spinning for me. My mind rolled like anything. I felt as if I had slipped deep into a river with my all organs tingling. My heart collapsed deep into a grave depression and remorse, not on whether what he was narrating to me was a truth or a story because he had his own axe to grind, but the idea that, if true, then it was wrong of me to live even for a second with a person who had killed the father of my two kids and made them orphans. Insecurities overwhelmed me. Doubts clustered around my vision. Being incandescent with revenge, I was hardly able to keep my balance at that boiling point of time.

Glowing with rage, finding my pieces of existence shattered and scattered, I started to reassemble them into myself. I tried to be able to regain my lost strength. It was, indeed, a challenge of its own type, quite unique for me. But my inner goddess made me realise that I had to not lose my composition and might come back to myself! I did it after straining my every nerve. Now was the time I reached the state of mind that enough was enough! I had suffered beyond repair without any fault or without any sin on my part. It became alarmingly clear to me that my all rack and ruins were because of my primary sin of being a woman in a society in which I was destined to be born and grow up.

However, I knew full well that my power of being a woman comes with negation of such perception of woman being a sin. I was to fight and reject it. I was to live with the belief that being a woman was a blessing at least for me. I realized that if I started buying the idea of woman being a sign of sin as well as a symbol of misfortune, I would not win the war of perceptions which I was prepared to wage in a deadly way; a warfare which could render me shelter less and all alone to sustain my life.

Unlike criminals and gangsters who were lethally armed with lethal weaponry, I was barely unarmed. My greatest of all weapons was my faith in myself. My determination to stand against all odds was my inexhaustible ammunition and my belief in my innocence gave me enough strength and vigour to enter into a fight for survival. I kept on trying to understand the sneaky tricks and clandestine crimes of Meeral in order to know about the secrets of Waqar's murder. One day Meeral confessed having been involved in killing Waqar, my ex-husband. He further explained the motive of this murder, admitting that, after seeing me for the first time; he fell in love with me and resolved to bring me into his life by hook or by crook. As it was impossible by hook, he opted for crook means. Therefore, he masterminded all the incidents of trapping us in the kidnap crisis, and that innocent kidnapped man, who was kept with us and who talked to his family from my cell phone, was not involved in informing the police; rather, Meeral had prepared the script and staged the drama of the police encounter.

# Chapter Six

I was a female, unlettered, unarmed and alone, trying to settle my scores with a pernicious criminal who was wanted by the government and law enforcing agencies. Even law enforcement agencies were helpless to arrest him. But then I was changed. My concepts were redefined. My notions found new versions. My motives added new meaning to themselves. At that time, my focus was not only freedom but also revenge. Requiting the abuse and sting caused by Meeral was tied to my freedom from the shackles of the system, which had long entrapped me in a vicious circle of male-dominated culture of violence and high-handedness.

I was not a good planner, nor yet an accomplished conspirator. But since the day I came to know about the facts associated with the killing of my ex-husband, I began to cudgel my brains to do something to attain freedom, which would be possible only after Meeral was jailed or eliminated. Meeral being brought to justice was the prime be-all and end-all of my life then.

A year after I determined to balance the account of emotions with Meeral, I heard of a chief cop who had been posted as district police officer (DPO) in Ghotki. His name was Shah Haq. DPO Shah Haq, meaning 'king of justice', was reportedly a one-man army and had a reputation for eliminating many outlaws in police encounters. And the day he joined our district, all criminals, including Meeral, began to feel scared and insecure. After his joining we never stayed at one place more than twelve hours but kept on shifting places within the island. The chief cop began to eliminate criminals and the message came to Meeral that the cop was desperate to engage in a deadly armed showdown with him and his gang. Meeral was reluctant to accept the challenge and was avoiding it. However, they stopped committing crimes and tried to survive on extortion money.

One day after being fed up with transitory stays at different places Meeral shifted us to an adjacent district called Kashmor where things were better for outlaws as most of the police was hand-in-glove with these gangs who used to share their criminal earnings with them. So, finding it safe, they shifted us all to a new place, similar in earthly conditions but different in legal jurisdictions.

At this moment, my mind began to picture a plan to get Meeral down. For that purpose, I got the cell number of a newly-posted chief cop who could be helpful for me and for many others, to get rid of all that was going on. I managed this through a criminal from Rahim Yar Khan who had revealed the secret of my ex-husband's murder to me. It was not a big deal to find the cell number because almost all the gangsters used to keep the numbers of all good and bad cops for different purposes.

One day I was alone. I made a call to the chief cop. I introduced myself to him. Then I explained the reasons as to why I had contacted him. Initially, he had many suspicions and kept on questioning me as if he was to appoint me to the police department but after a long and exhaustive telephone call, I made him realize that I really meant what I was saying. He slowly began to believe and to trust me.

The chief cop, Shah Haq, was a professional guy and despite many doubts, he never wanted to lose contact with an informer, who was asking nothing of him except genuine help and assistance. I kept an uninterrupted communication with him. He was never in a hurry. But I was, because I knew the cop could be transferred and no one knew what kind of guy would replace him. Good cops do not stay long in their positions due to the power of criminal and political nexus in our country.

One day a kidnapped foreigner named Tommy Jack was sold to Meeral by some kidnappers for getting a deal with the party struck through him. Tommy Jack was reportedly a UN employee based in the city of Sukkur in Sindh. Ransom demands were high. Meeral was a greedy soul and he bought the kidnapped man for a handsome amount and was desperate for everything related to him. The Sukkur police were under tremendous pressure for the release of the UN employee by any means. International pressure was also mounting on the Pakistani government. The chief cop of Ghotki district was not directly linked to this kidnapping case, nor was the camp where the kidnapped man was being kept within the jurisdiction of Ghotki. That was rather a third district, as the person had been kidnapped from Sukkur district and was being kept in Kashmor district. But the government tasked the chief cop, the police head of Ghotki district, to solve this case by any means, as the chief cop was considered as a hard taskmaster in his department. Such was his reputation.

The chief cop, Shah Haq, called me and enquired about the developments in the foreigner's case. I wanted to be loyal

31

to him and to pass on correct information. However, I was not fully aware of what exactly was going on in criminal circles in terms of the kidnapped foreigner's custody and deals. But I confirmed that the kidnapped foreigner was with the gang of Meeral but he was not keeping the kidnapped man at home or nearby. The kidnapped man's custody location was kept a secret. Only a few criminals had the knowledge; they were those who were deployed as day and night watchers to keep an eye on him and also those who used to bring food and medicine for the kidnapped man. It was later revealed that the kidnapped man was suffering from chronic diabetes. So he could not manage to survive without medicines and insulin.

When I came to know this, I updated the chief cop. The chief spread his spies to monitor the nearby medical stores. The chief also asked me how the medicines were purchased without prescription! After a little information-gathering, I came to know about a person who used to bring the medicines for the kidnapped man. He was a police constable.

The police constable, some in criminal circles said, did not know about the actual story of who was using the tablets. Besides this, I came to know that the patient himself was writing his own prescription, as monitoring was very tight on medical stores and the chief cop had also got a sample of the handwriting of the kidnappee from his UN office and was following each and every transaction. Criminals were halfway ahead in smartness.

Criminals not only kept on changing who was buying but also changed the places or cities where they bought medicines for the kidnapped man. As ill luck would have it, one day they bought from Ghotki city. The chief was informed and the person who bought was again a police constable who was reportedly doing it in good faith. He was caught and the handwriting of the prescription matched that of Tommy.

On further interrogations, the arrested constable disclosed that he had a brother in Kashmor district who had requested him to buy those medicines for him and who had given him that prescription. Furthermore, the suspect constable also revealed that he was buying from Ghotki because his brother had told him that such medicines were not available at medical stores in Kashmor. After these disclosures, the constable made a call to his brother, named Rais, asking him to collect medicine because the constable, without letting them know about his arrest, had expressed his inability on grounds of his official duties to go to Kashmor and further hand over medicines to his brother.

The constable's brother rushed to Ghotki to collect the medicines. No sooner did he reach there than he was caught by the chief cop's team. After working on him the whole night, the interrogators found him a liar. The Ghotki police threatened to kill him and his constable brother if he failed to cooperate. The guy was a consummate criminal. He was not to be easily broken with traditional police tricks. During interrogation, he masterminded a plan to escape the police custody. Therefore, he expressed so many things that were true but with *mala fide* intentions to trap and harm the police force. He made a deal with the chief cop, saying that he could help only after he was released and accompanied by some of the chief's team members to the jungle, for getting the kidnapped man released.

The argument that the arrested criminal gave to the police was that too many police officers could endanger the kidnapped man and in case of a well-planned attack there were high chances of the kidnapped man being killed. Therefore, the chief cop kept criminal Rais's police constable brother as a guarantee, and gave him his three best officers who volunteered to go with him in the guise of criminals to get the kidnapped man released.

# Chapter Seven

The criminal named Rais who was released by the police and who was the brother of the constable in the custody of the chief cop took three soldiers to the hideouts where the gangsters were living and where the routes and pathways were very complicated. Only the criminals and some locals knew about them. The chief of police risked the lives of his soldiers. They themselves ran the risk of losing their lives. They came to the criminals in the guise of being members of a criminal gang of the adjoining province of Balochistan. They apparently went to buy the kidnapped man. It was commonplace that if one gang could not strike a handsome deal or found difficulties in ensuring the safe custody of the kidnapped person, they used to sell the abductee to other gangs.

Here the scenario was surrounded by serious doubts. Who were these new arrivals, who proclaimed themselves as criminal gangsters, and who had come to buy a very expensive abductee? How and where did they join Rais quite out of blue? How and on what grounds did they dare to reach the area where even locals were scared to come? Who might be behind them? Those were the questions which lit the fire of suspicions in the minds of the criminals, who had a lifetime of experience of dealing with the world of crime.

Above all, it was perhaps a blunder of the chief cop not to

resist the volunteers' decision to enter an environment loaded with risks and vulnerabilities. It was also the chief's mistake to trust Rais who was more loyal to his gang and crazier for money than for his constable brother and his life. The arrangements were being made for their board and dinner. Meeral told me to mix anaesthetic tablets in the meals of the guests. I asked him why. He told me, 'Just do what I say; do not ask questions, nor argue.'

Seeing my body language of reluctance, Meeral said he was just testing me. Anyway, I did not mix anaesthesia in food. But when the meal was ready, Meeral himself mixed anaesthesia in meal of suspect police party sent by Shah Haq. All three guests ate and slept well for next eight hours uninterrupted. I could not call the cop to inform him about developments as Meeral did not leave my room that night and I could not find any space to talk to the chief, though I was very much worried about the safety of his team members but I was helpless to do anything.

It came as an utter surprise that Rais had a different plan. Rais, due to pressure of the police having his brother in the custody of the chief, played very smart. He told Meeral about everything that happened to him when he went to collect medicines. It was decided by Meeral that, irrespective of what was going to happen to his brother officer, all three were to be killed and their weapons confiscated. At first, Rais assured Meeral for compliance but he did not kill police party because he feared that his brother constable would face same thing in return. It is rightly said: 'Blood is thicker than water'. But Rais, in order to save his constable brother in the custody of chief cop, hoodwinked Meeral by telling him a lie that he had killed all three and thrown their bodies in the river. He took their weapons and ammunitions to show Meeral compliance with his order. But he did not kill them; he threw their bodies in a boat as they had been given high doses of anaesthesia.

Now another wave of emotional storms began to play with my innate instinct of motherhood as well as womanhood, when Meeral decided to leave the place where we were living with the intent of escaping a possible showdown with the police in the wake of three police officers of the chief cop going missing. I was very much worried. I was worried for myself, for my kids, for the future of my daughter and son. I was also a bit nostalgic this time. I felt that everything was stopping me from leaving. I was tantalized by the wistfulness that my home, though made up of mud and wood, would feel lonely and desolate having been decoupled from me and sundered by the kidnap embroilment. The tree before my house, which had long provided me shade from the burning sun, was very sad. My buffalos, whose milk I used to feed my children, were weeping. The hand-pump, which provided us with filtered water, was getting dry and was very much worried as there was hardly anyone left to move it and get benefit from it. We all were to leave that humanely hostile environment and forsaken place with which we had developed a kind of nostalgic feelings. It was harder for normal human beings to stay there even for a single night.

The place where we lived was deep in river jungle where all kinds of anti-human species, including snakes, insects, non-purified edibles and drinkables, hostile jungle, hostile environment, no technologies, weapons, crime, tribal conflicts and so many other tensions dominated our daily life. Such were the conditions where death was a priority. This was, indeed, a condition where life had lost its charms. It had retreated against the baleful and sadistic forces.

Despite all the horrors we were living with and all the fears that prevailed, people like me had no fear at least from all those who never wanted to approach death and who wanted to save their lives. At least I was safe from the lovers of life who could never ever risk their lives to harm me and my family. Odds of life there served as our castles of protections and bases of our strength.

We were seeing our castles shattering, our walls falling, our weapons rusting, our determination debilitating, and our career of crime crippling. I was feeling it deep inside and full well because most of the script of misfortune and displacement was of my own writing. I was co-author of that manuscript of fighting the values that I thought I should. I presumed that I was born with a purpose of fighting the cult of kidnapping for ransom which had become a leading problem of peace and order in our society. For accomplishing this task in a dignified way, I, being a woman, had to be very smart to defeat the gang men in a systematic way. So, I stood up. I risked everything for it: my family, my kids, and myself.

I did not know anything as to what was in store for us ahead in a new place and a new life. I was quite unaware of and unable to predict the future.

There was only one thing that I nurtured while inching ahead in a game of apparent self-destruction; that was hope, to dismantle the bondage of the system by disempowering dominant pseudo elites and by sacking the usurpers of authority from the precipice of pomp and show, especially for the women of my area and of the world who dared not to ply with the dictates of the powerful in the society and to play to their tunes.

My own thought that animated my mettle was not in saying

but surely in doing them in a befitting way. More important thing to consider in this context is thinking of doing something rather than just saying for the sake of saying. I thought and I did it.

While I had heard lots of local folk-stories about hopes and high hopes which were never encouraging, their endings and lessons always came to a dead-end which suggested to us: 'never hope against hope'.

Never hoping against hope was something which was an alarm bell for always staying realistic and avoiding fantasies. But I was not only into the fantastic game of life. I was also into the game of woman's struggle against the deadly demons of culture, virulent vultures of state and fatal fiends of society. My task was much more daunting than the game of life only. I had an objective with a clear roadmap. I had lots of questions in my mind and whose answers I was to look for while living in an antipathetic system of society.

I thought I was more than merely a human being. I am called the 'better half'. But I am always treated as the worse half. I must prove my being better while facing and bearing that which a man can never. Doing all this demanded a great sacrifice by me – a sacrifice of loved ones. I was ready. I had made up my mind. I had gathered strength. I had regained power. I had steeled my resolve relying purely on what I myself actually was without expecting any outside assistance from anywhere and from anyone.

Through glooms and blooms of life, I had learnt that self-help is the best help and that the war is my own war – a war which I had to wage as a last resort to survive in a society, where I had grown up as a weaker vessel. No way! I never thought I was ever weaker. I always thought that I was the mother: the reservoir of true love and the root of humanity was none but me; the scriptwriter and architect of man's character and its strength was none but me; and the great men were ever born and grown by none but me; they were once in and with none but me. They very often asked none but me for prayer, love, and food for them.

'I am still with them, pray for them, love them, and make food for them,' so I always feel.

Having all these notions and beliefs in mind, I was very confident and composed but what was constantly breaking me was the fact that I was not getting my due but men always got something overdue. I was to live with this realization that my destination to stand at par with men was miles away.

I was the virtual guardian of the family, the household, the kids, the emotions, the feelings, the honour, the secrets and the colours in man's life. What my man held was his right of being my husband who in our sub-continental rituals is called undisputed earthly master (*Majazi Khuda*), inheriting an absolute right over me while I had in return many responsibilities.

However, the man never accepts a woman's being the symbol of strength and power.

# Chapter Eight

All said and stated here is not a story but an unclad truth of my circumstance.

Through all that, what I was very conscious to guard was my own entity, my own inner self and my own conscience, which was biting me deep inside to stand for what was right and to reject what was wrong. Keeping someone hostage was, indeed, a wrong act in my scheme of morals and I always used to imagine how it would feel if someone did this to me, or my kids. Very inhuman and very cruel it was to me. So I had decided to do something good for fellow beings while living and surviving even with criminals, who were the rejected lot of society and who violated the rules, laws and the morals of society.

In this regard, I was making every possible effort to know about the gangsters' plans to shift the kidnapped foreigner to some other place so that I could do something for his release. As the kidnapped man was a foreigner, I was not able to communicate with him, nor could he, due to the language barrier. Nor still had I ever seen him, as he was not kept at my home. And very important, I never wanted to repeat the same mistake which I made losing my ex-husband, Waqar. This time, I was a bit more intelligent and careful in all that. I wanted my exit to be very safe, not a risky one.

Good tidings began all around.

Meeral came to me very unexpectedly to discuss how to shift the foreigner, as due to overwhelming pressure from government and law-enforcement agencies, he did not want to run the risk of getting caught. So, he came up with the novel idea of shifting the kidnapped man to another place, which was not known to me. He had to keep me in the dark in this connection. He unearthed his secret plan to me saying that we would move in the guise of being a family and kids in a private car with only 9mm pistols so that the cops would not have any idea as to what was going on and who was going how and why. But Meeral did not have a car. He needed a taxi. He used me for getting a taxi as hardly anybody would be suspicious of me. So I was tasked for this and we had to leave in the next eight hours by any means, failing which we could land in trouble of an irreversible nature.

I had a few hours to work out all this and call a car. I, together with Meeral and my two kids and two other accomplices of my husband, were to travel with the kidnapped foreigner, who was to sit in the back central seat with dark glasses and eyes his eyes tied with scotch tape inside the glasses. I was to sit with my kids on the front seat opposite the driver. Meeral was not a driver so some accomplice was to drive. This was the plan.

I shared our journey plan with the chief cop. He understood it and agreed to send us a car in the garb of a private taxi with his driver. He sent a private car with a driver who was to keep the chief updated about the whereabouts of the kidnapped foreigner in case I could not respond due the presence of my family and husband and due to the fear of being caught red-handed for spying for the police.

Being an accomplished master of intrigue and crime tactics,

Meeral was smarter than the cops. When the car with the driver arrived, he obtained all documents, car and driving licence from the cop's driver and told him to stay with his men until he brought his car back. The car had a tracker and I told the chief about his man being left behind. So the chief cop followed the tracker already installed in the car sent to us by him. In addition to this, the police also went with the car information including white Corolla, petrol, automatic transmission, and 1998 model with registration # ABZ 424. The information of particulars of car and tracking helped police to a great extent to trace, locate and spot the suspect car.

Meeral had not much time and was happy that the driver of the alleged taxi was left behind and so felt safe. I did not know the details of the police plan nor did they share them. The police knew our originating point. They had deployed many policemen, in civvies and in private cars, on the routes connecting to the originating point. This time they were fully prepared. They saw this opportunity as the first and last, so they did not want to miss it this time.

As we left they saw us passing in front of them but they had perhaps been told that rash and indiscriminate firing could increase the chances of the kidnapped man getting hurt or killed. Besides this, my kids and I, being a vulnerable group, served as a shield against any police attack.

For the police this was an ideal situation where they knew what vehicle the target was moving in, who were the travelling members, who were the targets, whom to save and whom to hit, what to do, where and when. In fact, the heads of cops were clear in all this.

This was a blessing for the police, but for me it was deadly because not all of the police knew that I was helping them, except the chief cop, who might not have been able to brief each and every other cop.

I was in grave distress. My kids were under serious threat. We were in an imperilment because any mishandling of the situation meant death and so-called damn collateral damage. I was tense. My mouth got dry and my face turned pale. Everything of mine was at stake. I was seeing blood, cries, and dead bodies. I was very much in deep confusion as regards the information that I had leaked. The waves of ideas which were passing through my mind and the streams of possibilities that were hitting my conscience made me very uneasy and anxious to get things stopped or happening before these waves and streams were to shatter me.

On our way, when we took the main highway, every vehicle seemed to me as if the whole world knew that we were criminals; that we had committed a felony; that everyone knew that we had a hostage; and that everything under the sun was just waiting to catch us, arrest us and kill us. I was trying to get my kids to sleep.

At one point a police official on checkpoint gave our driver an indication to stop. Our driver stopped and directed me to pretend to be ill and going to hospital. The policeman was fully armed and our men were too. Every man sitting in the car, except the hostage and me, was armed and ready. If the police sensed anything wrong, the criminals were to open fire. In such a situation, we would definitely have been stormed with so many bullets. My heart plummeted to my stomach.

I started praying God for a safe exit. The policeman came and asked, 'Is everything fine? Where are you going at this odd time?'

I was weeping and told him, 'I am not feeling well and we

are going to an emergency hospital.' There were too many cars in line so the police cop understood and let us go. When our car started speeding away from the checkpoint, I sighed with relief. To our good luck, this police checkpoint was not part of the police team spread by DPO Shah Haq but just a routine check. Therefore, they let us go, considering us a family going to the doctor.

My being relaxed did not last long. A little way ahead on the highway, the police highway patrol was waiting. They knew and had information about our car. They did not indicate us to stop but started following us. Our driver doubted that the police would follow our car at 140 km per hour, so Meeral directed the driver to go slow, at 80 km per hour, to check whether the police were following us or going their own way.

As we slowed, the police van got slower and did not overtake us, making it clear that they were chasing us. This left the gangsters with two options: either to try to drive away at speed leaving the police far behind or to take some link road and leave the car.

They opted for the first option. They increased the speed and tried to reach 180 km per hour. The police were still following at break-neck speed but now we saw it was a private car not a police van. This made us confused whether it was a private car or carrying police officials in civvies. We got slower and so did the chasing car and then we sped up to the maximum speed. The car was following and trying to overtake at one point.

Our driver was not giving them space to overtake us. They tried to overrun us. This was a very dicey situation, indeed. There was a complete race. Police officials and our men both did not open fire. Both were observing care and caution to

45

avoid any mishap. Our men wanted to flee unhurt; so they, too, did not want to hurt or target any cop. Ultimately, after forty to fifty kilometres of a death-race, we saw more police and we understood it was more informed. But our driver had no option either to stop or to slow down the speed. Therefore, our driver made a full-fledged attempt to speed away.

I began to cry and pleaded with them to stop but they turned their guns to me and directed me to cry in front of the police loudly saying: 'save me, save me, they are kidnapping me.' I did that and the police did not open fire believing that the criminals had taken a family hostage and in case of indiscriminate firing they could hit the family. So the police followed us with great caution.

The police ultimately intercepted and fired on the tyre and our car lost balance and the driver slowly tried to stop it. And he did. The police put one van in front and another behind to control us. Meeral was sitting behind me. I told everyone not to risk anything as we were totally entrapped and overpowered.

But Meeral was a crime veteran of his time who had been dodging police for the last twenty years to escape his arrest. He became desperate. He never wanted the police to arrest him so easily. He opened the back door and fired on the cops sitting in the police van, seriously injuring one who he targeted while trying to flee into the crops of cotton. The police officials took a headshot with their sniper and he fell. He was down. We all raised our hands and got arrested.

When the captive Tommy saw the police, he started crying that he was a hostage. So the police also knew about him and took him to another car. I was arrested with two other criminals and Meeral was killed. The hostage was a foreigner and he was a victim so police believed him more than anyone else. Tommy stated to the police that the kids and the woman (me) were involved in keeping, feeding and transporting him from one place to another.

So I was booked in a case of kidnapping despite the fact that I helped the police. To some extent the chief of police tried to save me but he could not succumb to the pressure of diplomats and the government nor could he make them understand the actual facts about the whole crime-solving story but they were busy celebrating their victory and receiving cash awards from the government on their successful recovery of a high-profile hostage of international repute and stature.

Both in police investigations and also in court, the hostage gave statements against me and my kids as it was a fact that we lived there with criminals. And I was in a spousal relationship with a deceased gang leader, Meeral, though forcibly. Meeral was carrying reward money on his arrest, dead or alive. And also we used to feed the hostage sometimes, so he was right, at his end, in what he stated.

I was quite in the dark about the sequence of events following the recovery of the hostage. I tried to explain myself but nobody listened. I looked to the media but they were not clever enough to see my innocence and helplessness. I was also thinking that the cop, whom I helped to my own peril, would come to save me but I was not able to see him around. I was not able to see him thereafter when I was in police custody with my kids, whose already uncertain future had been clouded darkly with only the remotest chances of ever seeing any light of hope of regaining the lost chances of finding the fortune for them.

I saw no one around except my loneliness to fight the assaults on my fortune. I was alone. My kids were too young to do anything. Coming from criminals, now I had to face criminal justice agents, who appeared more callous, more ruthless and more polluted especially about my being a woman, and womanhood.

During interrogations, whatever they asked me I expressed my true colours, and avoided even white lies. I was saying what I had seen, observed, and what I thought was right and true. But my sermons fell on deaf and poisoned ears. After listening for hours, the detectives ended my conversation with the comments: 'What a beautiful and smart liar'. All my tales of truth were found to be tailor-made stories of falsehood by the men in uniform. On this attitude of the cops, my heart did not stop squeezing and bleeding.

One day, the interrogators had called the foreign hostage to ask me some questions in front of him and his translator. It was a very ruined room with two chairs and an old wooden table with hanging lights, to make the accused feel the awe and authority of the state and its laws, giving the impression of the aura of punishment.

I went in there handcuffed. Two lady police officials accompanied me. They started their queries. First the officer in charge of the interrogation team began to gaze with his eyebrows fluctuating up and down and his mouth movements left and right with teeth biting his lower lip. Finally, he broke the silence with very pinching words, uttering: 'So you are Hoor – the beautiful; what beauty you have! What can I call you? Should I call you a beautiful criminal? Should I take you as a beautiful prostitute to be used by the gangsters? Or should I understand you a useful item for the hostage service? Or should I classify you as a beautiful victim of the cruelties of the world?'

He further said: 'I can't take you to be a victim because

of your being in a marital relationship with a notorious kidnapper. Indeed, what my conscience suggests to me is to consider you as a professional, a criminal accomplice of the criminal gangster.'

His words worked as a sharp knife, cutting my whole existence and person inside into pieces. In this state of affairs, my mind rolled, taking me to a state where I found myself standing in front of God and asking him where He is. Why is there no one who understands my innocence and why there is no one whom I can tell that what happened in my world was not of my own choice but that I was made to live such a life of misery and helplessness! To whom should I tell the difference between choice and chance? Who would believe me and why? This was all I was cooking in my mind right at that moment.

But there in the interrogation room, the cat had just taken my tongue. I was speechless. I knew whatever I said was already declared as a 'beautiful lie'. When the detective's face turned beet-red, the lady constable speaking on my behalf said that I had revealed everything and now I was not feeling well. On this, the officer started questioning about me from the hostage who came up with all those things he saw and observed about me.

The hostage said he saw me when he was being shifted to other place. And further he told the detective that he had never seen me before, nor did he know who I was or what relation I had with anyone there. Then the detective asked me whether I had received any training regarding operating firearms or had I ever operated any weapon and if yes when and which weapon and why. I had nothing in my knowledge about weapons to share.

I denied having received any training or having operated

weapons but I admitted that I knew how to operate weapons, how to fire a gun, which I learnt seeing others doing that but I had never attempted it. During this, I fell on the ground due to custodial torture, weaknesses and tensions, which were cracking me inside uninterruptedly.

Then, I was taken to hospital.

# Chapter Nine

When I was revived back to consciousness, I found myself on a hospital bed. I was cuffed to the bed. The lady constable was there with her draconian face. I asked the hospital nurse next to the constable what had happened to me. She told me that I had undergone mental torture and sleeplessness of an acute nature. As a result, I was brought in a very serious condition to the hospital. In a state of serious dismay, I asked both of them why I did not die. Both watched each other's faces and expressed facial gestures of utter surprise.

The hospital nurse asked the police lady about my criminal background. The police lady told her I was a big criminal associated with the most dangerous criminal gangs who kidnapped and killed people for money. The hospital staff became scared of me and I found them very indifferent to me and about my hospital care thereafter. I started feeling, why should I blame men for treating me fairly and well, since both the police lady and hospital nurse were females but were hardly willing to listen to anything different from what they were being told by male-dominated narratives within their society and culture. Truly, I found them victims of the same 'normative engineering' as I was feeling about myself.

On that hospital bed, I was undergoing a war of ideas almost overlapping and contrasting with what I had witnessed all through the ordeal I had fallen in. I was speaking to myself. I was very surprised, being an unlettered woman, that I heard people saying: 'Education makes people perfect and true human beings'. Since the females I interacted with during my custody were said to be well-read ladies, holding academic degrees and government offices, I hardly found anything of the ilk which could have made me think that I was lacking. Rather I was a bit confident that I understood the people and the world much better than these so-called educated lot mandated to correct wrongdoings and misdeeds in society.

Where I was born and how I grew up, I never thought it was my fault. This was perhaps purely because of chance and luck. It was something beyond human reach. How I was and where I was, however, was my fault, and I admitted it beyond any iota of regret. I would have been at some better place, had I made a little effort in a right direction. Lack of initiative dragged me in a vicious circle, which I knew was destined to destroy me and to ruin all associated with me.

The idea of doing something meaningful in time, which I had badly failed to do, always raised a question mark in me about my lack of initiative.

Sometimes, I thought I should have gone to school but I was a kid and there was no school in my neighbourhood. Very often an idea appealed to me that I must have received some education at home. I was a female, unlettered initially, and hailed from a very humble family background. However, I resisted male-dominance and a culture of gender discrimination in an educated manner.

For example I should have resisted my marriage which had been contracted with a person whom I had not seen before; I was quite unaware as to who he was, what he used to do, what he looked like, what reputation he enjoyed and whether I could adjust or not, and so on. But I had no choice at all other than being complacent with what my parents had decided, even if I had been told that my parents received only 25000 rupees from the groom's family as compensation for agreeing to allow me to marry my first husband, Waqar. This money was given to my parents for meeting wedding expenses. Other things had already been decided by the *Jirga* about my father Sakhie and my in-laws, the family of Alan, some twelve years back. My father, Sakhie, paid me in compensation for his sins to save his life from honour revenge of Alan.

Due to getting me as an indemnity from their arch foes, Waqar and his family including Alan never ever gave me the respect that they should have given me. They always treated me like they treated their cattle and other things of sale and purchase. There was hardly any intimacy ever developed which was needed to weld the wedding bond well. I used to feel that they had just bought me to use me as a household servant, a sexual tool and a child-bearing machine.

The circumstances that surrounded my second marriage were almost similar. A man who had killed my husband married me at gunpoint. I had no option but to find a refuge, a shelter not for me but also for my two kids who were made fatherless. A man who had killed their father was to act as their father and my kids were to treat him accordingly.

So is the tale of my torments and so is the format of my fortune.

The reason why I got wedded with the notorious outlaw and killer of the father of my kids was to accept him in order to get the dust of crisis settled for the time being and to get shelter for my kids. That I did at least at the cost of ten years imprisonment with both of my kids. There was no gentleman to accept me. Perhaps destiny's designer had not willed it this way; but I was a victim of the system.

Despite this apparent mayhem, I was quite contented with what I had done in terms of giving information to the police and consequently bringing about the elimination of the most notorious criminal of his time who was quite unprecedented in terms of savagery, barbarity, criminality, inhumanity and sanguineness of his crimes. At least, I was contended that many innocent people, who were yet to fall victim to the savagery of Meeral, had been saved due to his elimination.

The man who killed my ex-husband Waqar and married me was cloven-footed. His notoriety and barbarity were well known; and this human locust had annihilated many homes and families just to overpower for prominence, lust and money. He was well connected with the power brokers in society who were called local notables and who were wielding authority at the cost of the communities they were in charge of on a tribal basis. He had some accomplices in the police and in politics also.

However, the day he went down, nobody ever bothered about him afterwards. Everything about him was gone with the wind the very moment of his leaving this world, as if he was never born! Therefore, though in jail and sentenced, I found jail a better place than where I had been since my birth. In jail, there was a disciplined schedule; we used every second of our life in jail; we remembered it; and sometimes utilized it for education there. So, jail proved a blessing in disguise for me.

Taking my imprisonment as an advantage, I started my vocational education there. There were no schools for juveniles but I requested help from our superintendent jail lady,

Roheena, who was head of the female sections of jail, so both I and my daughter fell in her administrative and supervisory control. She was a graceful lady and managed a tutor for my daughter Zuhra for private education. She found a lady teacher named Ambreen. She kept on educating me and my daughter. I also continued with my vocational as well as conventional education.

However, my son, Mehar, could not get education due to the bad conditions at the boy's section of juvenile jail. I could not take care of him the way I did for my daughter, being in the same compound. But fortunately he had already passed six classes, as he was a boy so he successfully managed it. For a pretty good time he developed a psychologically complex character. I wanted to do something for him but I could not, as I was an inmate and so had my limitations. But being a mother I made every possible effort to stitch meanings to my son's life; though all my efforts ended in smoke to heal the scars of time and circumstances he was in.

# Chapter Ten

My daughter Zuhra was very good at drawing and singing. Her teacher, Ambreen, told me she could work wonders in acting and singing. I asked the teacher, 'Couldn't she get an education to find a job when out of jail?'

Ambreen said, 'A job does not mean a government job or a monthly salary; even a proper housewife has a job of keeping a home. So, the best thing I suggest is let her be free to explore her in a better way so that she can locate her talents.'

The teacher continued, 'Singing, dancing and modelling are not ordinary things. If she clicks, the world will be after her, even me and you.'

The teacher's comments meant a lot to me. My daughter was growing. She was about to kill her childhood. The day she started worrying about what she would be doing tomorrow to make both ends meet, she would definitely be saying goodbye to her innocence that I will always be hell-bent on getting her to carry through all the thick and thin of life. Innocence and tenderness are parts of the identity of being a woman. It is our ornament of femininity. Protecting her innocence meant much more to me than worrying for her future jobs and earnings. That I did to the extent of a wounded mother lion looking after her kids.

I am a woman. I know what it is like being a woman in

all its essence and all its implications. I feel the sensitivity of a woman to her vulnerabilities. I can imagine the pain of man's evil eye when she goes to do something outside her home. Things can get hellish when you have a beautiful face which, at times, gives you pleasure that you are different and a centre of attention; but beauty does not always pay. It is, indeed, very taxing too.

Like me, my daughter had a beautiful appearance and features. She was completely in balance and proportion. The community my child lived in lacked humanity and civilization. Equally bad were the conditions of jail. Learning mannerism appeared a distant dream.

I used to teach my own versions of humanity to my daughter, 'Your humanity is your independence of thought, freedom of action and liberty of conscience. Your humanity is your originality because in essence it stands the same but in form it varies from one person to another, constituting the very base of your individuality as the level, degree and the magnitude of being free vary from one person to another.'

The next day I met Ambreen again. She asked me about my experience of jail, 'How is life in jail? What do you feel being here with kids?'

I opened my heart to her. 'It is extremely hard for a child or a teen to live peacefully and perfectly without a home. Jail is hell, not home. Home is heaven, where especially a woman feels safe, happy, active, creative, stable and at her best.'

Flipping further pages of my heart, I reflected: 'Homelessness is the strictest of all penalties, even in a proverbial sense. You, being a free lady, can't really imagine how haunting and how soul-pulling jails and imprisonments are even for real culprits, who are convicted for what they have committed. And for those innocents who have done nothing wrong but become enchained here, it is a more bewailing predicament.'

Ambreen further asked me, 'Is it true for both men and women?' On this I spoke out my mind in this way:

'It is painful even for a man, but I am talking about women, who are innocent; it is a gross violation of the values of justice, equity, fairplay, and humanity. Jail sentence to me with my two children really irritated me beyond mention. We know we have committed no crime; we know, being female and poor, I and my daughter are the weakest and most vulnerable social group; we feel that the state's authority or power works only on helpless people like us, who have no resources to buy freedom.'

The teacher's jaw dropped at my solid comment on the cost of freedom and she asked, 'How about buying freedom? Is it a commodity available in streets and malls?'

I very crisply responded to her, 'Dear, freedom is not available for free! Everyone has to pay, one way or the other, to the monopolist of the system.'

I invited her attention to my personal experience of witnessing the incident in these words to further clear my inner itching about confinement. I narrated:

'One day, after the court hearing, we were on our way back to jail from the court, when my eyes caught a glimpse of a street beggar scenario wherein a beggar woman with two kids and a husband was sitting on a footpath eating a meal as beggars are seen to do everywhere; for a while my heart started bleeding but after a while I realized that the beggar woman was better than me, though she was poor and homeless. Her entire world was at least there with her. She was free to do or not to do anything. At least she was not at the mercy of anyone; at least she had no blame on her; at least her family was with her; at least she was breathing in fresh air; at least she was not uncertain as to what was going to happen in the next moment; and at least she had a husband to protect her when she felt aggrieved.'

I further connected my life conditions to that of a beggar woman by registering my grievances in this way:

'On the contrary, I was alone. My family was destroyed. I was without husband. I did not have my kids with me. I was not in a position to make early breakfasts for them. I was always in a state of my heart missing a beat as to whether my kids who were kept in different compartments had taken a meal or gone hungry all the time. This thought of my helplessness kept my inner peace undermined and my claims of behaving like a mother nullified. Such helplessness of proving my motherhood was shattering my womanhood; it was more disheartening than my inability to prove my innocence.'

All this together pushed me to a state of mind where I started wondering how long I would be able to continue this war with myself and with my conscience. This was haunting.

But for the sake of Zuhra, my daughter, Mehar, my son, and for my fellow women, I was to survive all ordeals. I was also to fight my case of life, my case of gender, my case of poverty, my case of helplessness, my case of freedom, my case of innocence, and my case of justice.

While preparing to fight all of these cases, the more startling for me was not what was happening with me and many others like me; but the apathy and indifference of our institutions of the state as well as of society, which were very much in full swing with satisfaction that they were discharging their lawful duties full well by prosecuting and punishing those who, in their view, were found guilty. On this my heart always used to creep into my mouth.

Ambreen's curiosity to listen to me and my vision killed her shyness. She further picked two words: innocence and freedom, and wanted a more detailed explanation from me. I did give more reflections on the theme in focus, this way:

'I have not read anywhere as I am uneducated but being an innocent inmate, I have felt that people can live without eating, drinking and money but they cannot survive without freedom and justice; and the system of governance which fails to ensure justice and freedom loses the ethics of existence and bases of legitimacy, giving birth to a serious crisis of statehood.'

Further scratching the essence of ideas from the bottom of my heart, I drew this sketch of feelings:

'The crisis of statehood results in social unrest which in turn could progress into uprising and then anarchy. Society, in anarchy, loses its social order, causing serious law and order issues. When anarchy develops into disorder and lawlessness, the concerned institutions lose their justification to perpetuate and people begin to discuss their replacement with new ones with new norms and with new visions.'

I went ahead,

'Such cataclysmic changes are always defined as revolution which takes away everything except a new thinking. New social values are shaped with the flag of freedom hovering over everything. Our country's political system is in a serious crisis of statehood and no one knows where the system based on injustice does and tyranny takes us!'

Ambreen's pin-drop silence was very revealing that she needed to know more. However, I kept on digging ideas from the roots of my consciousness and experience:

'Wherever the system goes, but we are to live with the reality that we are denied our freedom; we are prosecuted, tried, and sentenced to ten-year terms in jail. The revolutions, the changes of values hardly mean anything to us as right at the moment; we are hard hit by the bitter truths of our system.'

# Chapter Eleven

Being imprisoned is the worst of all human feelings. Even if someone deserves to be imprisoned for his felonies, everyone always resists it, avoids it, evades it, negates it and also hates it because to me the most difficult to negotiate and to leverage is my freedom for anything, however sweet and dear it may be to me. Freedom is, therefore, dearer than dearest and sweeter than sweetest, to me.

The hall of women in the jail where I was accommodated was not better than the mud houses with wooden roofs where I had been living since my childhood. You might laugh at my observation but it was the fact. Let me bring out my notion: 'It is always the feeling of a dweller, and not the strength of structure of building that really matters to the happiness of the humans. A free man or woman even having no house feels much better than the person whose home is declared jail and he or she is said to be under home-arrest.'

The essence of my faith in freedom goes like this: 'Freedom for human beings, to me, is not merely a virtue, a state of affairs, a way of life, a road to dignity, a source of survival, a path to progress, a certificate for creativity, a proof of genius, a gateway to knowledge, an insurance of faith, the most cherished human feeling but also an identity of superior human creatures.'

However, jail life was very unbearable because this was a

very old and very hot building. Secondly, here more than thirty women were boarded with me in a single compound. Thirdly, being so heavily crowded and having filthy latrines inside the rooms and with the roof half open, the hall remained smelly almost all the time. Fourthly, it was really very difficult to eat a meal when inside the hall; but it was the place where all we females used to do everything in our daily routine, including eating, drinking, sleeping, taking baths, going to attend calls of nature and everything, so it remained all the time messy, unhygienic and smelly, causing many diseases.

Our homes, though very humble, were tidy and clean with clean air flowing in rural areas, which was never thick with smoke as is the case here in cities and also with clean and hygienic water from inside the earth, not from a water supply as is the case here in urban centres.

Besides very bad living conditions inside, some old inmates used to talk about some very bad times in jail where the jail administration, being hand-in-glove with the powerful and wealthy elites of the society, used to run the women's jail like a brothel house.

In simple words, female jails were brothel industries as young women and teens used to get imprisoned for their minor or major crimes and they, with their very tender minds, in their bid to earn money for buying freedom, fell as easy prey to the whims of vultures inside and outside the jail.

For this reason in mind, I feared being a victim, and for my daughter, who had reached puberty, killing her infancy and innocence. I became afraid even of my own shadow.

Five years had passed. Everything had drastically changed inside the jail and outside in society. The new elected government was in power. People had elected them for improving affairs, which were turning worse every other day. Every day, terrorist incidents were taking place in every nook and corner of my country and this was being reported in the media, which was my daily routine to see with cooperation of Maheen, a lady constable. The situation was grim. There were hardly any solutions at hand. Allegations and deliberations were the order of the day on TV talk shows.

Good for me was my personal progress. I had passed my eighth class privately, learning to read and to write well.

I and my daughter had learnt to read and write in those five years. Now she was seventeen and with me. She had grown into a complete lady. I was somehow content because of her being with me in the same hall of women. We both were declared as very good inmates who always cooperated and followed the orders of the jail administration in terms of implementing their decisions in daily routines. I not only did my best to avail myself of the opportunity to learn but I also behaved in a civilized manner earning respect and regard for me. My credentials helped me to talk for others who were either new or unwilling or rather reluctant inmates.

As I had entered the jail with a clear concept of completing the term because of being a resourceless widow having two children, I was to accept what destiny had willed for me. With patience and belief it was in my mind that there will be my day, one day. I had a faith in myself that even though I was a woman, I would prove that I was a very useful citizen of this country. I was a very good mother and in addition had acted as a father and friend also. I believed that I would make my way to success and recognition.

Being a very good and cooperative inmate had many advantages that I was not aware of initially but what I did during my imprisonment was natural. What I thought was right, I always did. My good conduct throughout earned me a good reputation. Besides this, during the ordeal of imprisonment and freedom-free or liberty-locked moments that I was there in jail to spend, I discovered myself and my true colours. What I faced worked like a mirror to see my own person inside me, to see where the faults lay in me and to explore my strengths. Fault-finding enabled me to overcome my own weaknesses and to conquer my own fears which I did very successfully.

During my initial years I came to the conclusion that there was nothing to gain in crying and complaining for innocence as the time of trials was over. The time of execution of the orders had begun. Best compliance with such orders, considering court as your correcting institution and jails as your rehabilitating places, was the best course left to follow. I did it the same way.

The fact which always emerged as a blessing in disguise was my learning during the term. With the background I was from I would never ever have been able to learn what I learnt in jail, had I not been sent to jail. It proved a very strict boarding school for me. My person inside had never allowed any criminality to grow in me! So, the question of psychological rehabilitation was irrelevant and I didn't want to touch things that were not part of my stay in jail and that neither I felt nor did I observe.

In addition to it, imprisonment deprived me of my inborn right of freedom, but offered me a protection that kept me and my innocence intact.

Now I had learnt to earn and survive. I had learnt how to interact with fellow urban women. I had also developed a pretty good understanding of the problems and wishes of the women.

I also came to know of womanhood and gender-hood in true letter and spirit. I had never seen crowds of women before with such a large variety of guilty as well as innocent natures, with different backgrounds and with everyone telling her own story.

I found jail to be a truth house and a very fertile place for intelligence gathering of all types. Jails have also a great capacity to work as emotion industries to assemble characters and to weld human relationships in such intimate ways.

In those five years I had become not only a good listener but also a good story teller and a good story narrator. Jail was a place of many real stories. Interestingly, no inmate ever tried to tell a fictitious or concocted story which, to him or to her, was nothing more than a waste of everyone's time with no gains to anyone at all.

The other reason for speaking the truth with the partners in punishment was the natural human emotional attachment of bad times. I can never forget my bad timers and I can never ever forget every Tom, Dick, and Harry who heard me and my tales of torment, taking an interest in my world even for a while out of the time that was, indeed, theirs. I cannot really forget those moments.

Very rewarding, being in jail, proved my developing of relations with co-inmates because we became no less than as thick as thieves for one another. Bad timers, to me, are all timers. The friends in pain are friends forever.

In pain your creativity comes out, your expression improves, your acumen sharpens, your understanding power enhances, and you become responsive as well as responsible in your life, discovering your real potential as a thinking and feeling animal. I thought exceptionally and I felt pervasively during my ordeal.

The relationships not only developed, but developed very genuinely, very intimately, very meaningfully and very powerfully, and lasted long. This is what I have learnt and this is what I have seen others have gained, being in jail.

Formal imprisonment, for whatever reason, changed my impressions about different segments of our society. Initially, before entering jail, I had an impression of only illiterate criminals and simple villagers whom I had spent my life with. Illiteracy and crime, I always abhorred. While the simplicity and originality of people from villages I always rated highly in my scheme of morals and ethics.

When I came out of my home and was arrested, my impression of the police being better than the criminals was badly dented during my interaction with them in long interrogations. The language they used to extract information from me was worse than the criminals. The way they treated me, as a woman, needs to be listed in *The Guinness Book of World Records*.

My perception of police as protectors changed. Interrogators were fully exposed to me. They were mediocre but they feigned knowledge of everything under the sun. The fact remains these poor cops had their own worries and were a severely opinionated lot who needed to free themselves from what they think is the last word on earth. There are more words with meanings and with truths; the cops must be educated in that.

I also had some more new impressions developed after my interactions with the people from different walks of life. These include people linked with information, media, bar, bench, law and order, human rights, development and democracy. Most of these people were very noble and they really were doing marvels for improving the lot of the people with problems. No doubt, some of the cops were also gems. However, in all fields the good people with high moral values were less in numbers.

Flirting with women, the man considers his inherent right as if he is born with capacity of loving every woman on earth. This tendency dominates and becomes alarmingly visible if the woman happens to be beautiful. There are very few and far between who try their utmost to control their impulse with a view to leaving a good first impression and keeping something flirty for the next meeting. Such are rare entities who at least control their nerves and passions.

Moreover, the mediocre man speaks more through his body language than through his tongue. His pretentions of silence, of grace, of gentleness and of control crash the very moment he gets even a misleading gesture from the female.

Whether the woman likes the man or not he struggles to maintain his monopoly on love, romance and everything. He believes that since he likes to talk to woman so woman should talk to him without thinking whether the woman he intends to talk to is interested or not, or likes him or not.

# Chapter Twelve

Having had some multi-faceted learning and exposure to almost all segments of society, I made a big but a sweet mistake. The ghost of romance which was hidden in my personality but which no body had been able to locate, and which was awaiting its reflector, came out of the bottle. I fell in love with an unseen, unspoken, little known to me story-writer of the day.

I never had any interaction with him. I started liking and loving him in the fifth year of my imprisonment. It was so because his ideas were the forces which accompanied me to kill my loneliness in jail. I came to know him through his stories, which he used to write in a female magazine.

I found myself in his stories. I saw my shadow and reflections in the female characters of his stories. He used to highlight the aspects of women's woes that I had almost undergone. Besides all this, what really moved my heart was his style of writing which was simple, effective and dynamic? His moral of the story was always rocking, surprising, and enthralling.

Through reading his stories, the feeling of cherishing someone as my hero began to grow in my heart. I betrayed myself and my solitude.

Page 101 of my diary, which I wrote in jail and which I want to share here, reads:

'I was in complete darkness about what love is and how it feels to be in love with someone. The candle of love is lit in my life by letters. It is not until I learnt to read and write that the world was fully exposed to me and that its finest essence has come out like a glittering hope, germinating the desire to survive the crisis of fate and sustain the ordeals of life so caused by the system.

Love and I now know each other; it was a stranger to me before. Love minimizes my loneliness; it packs up the sheets of isolation rolled on myself for a long time. Love protects me against all temptations of life; it cultivates humility and guards integrity. Love teaches me what is important in life to keep and what garbage to throw in the dustbin is. I love my own company because I believe I belong to someone; I owe someone something very special. I have given myself to one who claims to love me. Until he comes to know that someone loves him, I will keep loving myself because it's my very sincere friend who worries when I find myself in the middle of some trouble and I also worry for its whiter than white entity. I feel pleased and joyful when I am happy and comfortable. My own link to myself cracks my arrogance and enlightens my innocence to the core.

I am tired of being concerned for those who had never ever taken care of me. I have been through troubles and torments of high magnitude. Nothing but only my solitude has stood by me in all the thick and thin of life. Thriving on double standards, hypocrisy, duality, duplicity, artificiality, is beyond my possibilities.

For many this may be the code of success and art of winning in life; but for me success or victory in truer terms does not come with fake smiles, concocted stories, and artificial praises. My key to success is with the satisfaction of my inner goddess. In that are my peace, my solace, and my eternal happiness.

I am of the strong view that in love, blood relation does not count the way the charm of matching of minds and hearts does.

I can no longer wait for those who are here to make me their wife, or for those who do not appeal to me, nor yet for those who do not need me. Now I can't negotiate my emotions, passions, and freedoms nor could I deal in myself. Now I will track the trail of the music of my heart and frequency of my feelings. It is enough for now.'

My marital and romantic part of life is very unique and of its own kind. My words may not justify the way it has been but surely I am here to let you know what has been happening to me and my heart over the years. Now let us gauge the heart-meter. Let us have a word with the world of love for which we all are here on the earth to learn and to grow.

Elderly people used to tell us stories of kings and queens in our childhood. In those stories, one thing was always prominent, either the power game or the emotion game. As per the emotion game, every male and female happens to face love at least once in a lifetime.

However, some are unfortunate enough to have many turns and many innings in love. Such restless souls keep on searching their mates until they stop where they find their frequencies match, their minds mix and their hearts heat up together.

My story of my marriage and my story of love go inversely. They never converge.

My story of marriage begins when I had not opened my eyes. I do not refer to pre-destiny. I refer to a deal of my marriage when I was not yet born. In our part of the world where my parents were living, there was a very old custom and cult of killing woman in the name of honour. According to this cult, womenfolk are considered as the honour symbol of family and tribe.

If any woman was suspected of having any extramarital or sexual relationships or were running any love affair they were declared 'morally black' and were liable to be killed. Their killing was believed to purify the tribe, worked as a deterrent for other women and also restored the, so-called, lost honour to the family.

My father Sakhie was blamed by a rival tribe, with whom our land disputes were going on long before I was born, for having alleged illicit relations with the woman of another tribe, which had brought a bad name to their family.

After a few years, Mr. Sakhie was blessed with a baby girl. That was none but me! As a consequence of *Jirga* decision I was to marry a person without my consent. So I can say that, 'I was wedded before I had seen the world'. In marriage I had no choice. I was not given any option. So I was born with a damning flaw of my freedom already mortgaged by the unfair system of my society.

That was the first assault on my freedom, which I bore with courage and confidence though I knew full well that something seriously wrong was being done to me.

So I was wedded to Waqar who was the brother of the murdered lady. On my wedding I was only ten years old and had not attained the age of puberty, which is *sine qua non* for a marriage.

Due to my early forced marriage with a fully grown man of twenty-eight years, I could hardly understand the true meaning of marriage. I was immature. I was under age. I was unaware of what marriage was all about! I did not even know why I was being made a scapegoat. None of my family members including my mother disclosed to me anything about the background of this marriage.

On my marriage as far as I remember, my father had his lips fully zipped owing to his inner regrets of sacrificing his little daughter to save his life and hide his sins. I was being punished for the sins and wrongdoings of my father. My mother's eyes were showering; she was crying like anything. I asked my mother why she was crying, because I was being told by everyone that 'marriage means happiness while death means grief'.

It was an event of happiness yet everyone in my family were either weeping, or keeping silence, or even collapsing to the core.

Because they knew what was going to happen to me soon after the marriage was over. My mother was speechless yet she was not in a position to do anything. I just sensed that something was seriously wrong. But she was feeling pity on me but was not intentionally scaring me.

After exactly two years of my marriage with Waqar, who liked me because of my tenderness and innocence, I came to know exactly the reasons and background behind the morning at the time of my marriage.

When I was wedded, my husband remained rude and reluctant with me in everything because he felt that his sister had been killed because of my father. Therefore, he always considered me to be from his enemy's family.

As I was too young so he did not express himself full well but he remained carefree, wild and violent even in lovemaking, talking and also thinking about me. Perhaps, what I felt was him being an uneducated person full of all kinds of possible biases, was actually his trying to seek revenge for his sister in molesting, abusing and misusing me as if I was war booty.

Despite all his highhandedness, I realized and understood why he was so rude with me and why he continued his reign of harassment and victimization of me.

In four years of all kinds of hardships I was able to locate my husband's pulse and then played with him very cleverly to fix him so that I could reduce my own agonies. What I discovered was that Waqar liked me, as I was very beautiful. This was what my mirror used to tell me. This was also how many girls praised me.

I was irresistible for Waqar. I was to tantalize him for everything; so for one or the other reason I had to keep him waiting for everything marital so one day he lost his nerves and tried to be violent and offensive with me but I resisted him tooth and nail. Finally, I succeeded in keeping him away.

Slowly he tried to change himself. He was ultimately backed to his mettle. Now he confessed his having an emotional attachment with me. I sarcastically responded to him in a way as if I disbelieved what he was talking about.

After that understanding we had two children but Waqar's mother Aleena was never on good terms with me and she always wanted Waqar to settle their old score of their murdered daughter by keeping me tense and unhappy. Her magic did not work at all. Gone were the days of my persecutions. My heart grew harder to face any eventuality.

I was hard hit by my immaturity and by my own innocence at all stages. What saved me during all the odd days was my own faith in myself. I was confident and composed even when

I was subjected to the worst masculine torture during my early tender age.

I had in mind an unshaken belief in myself that one day it would be my day and that day I would fully overcome what was being done to me. I was quite sure that one day I would be calling the tunes.

It was the time when I was convinced by my inner person to draw a line in the sand and to resist full well the co-existence of woes in my life. In order to achieve all this I needed a courage and boldness that I gathered by knowing myself and my innate powers of being a woman.

During self-understanding of my own self, I came to know that being a woman was not an ordinary thing for me; it was special; it was a privilege; it was an honour, it was beautiful and it was great.

Nothing is like the feeling when people around me used to say that I was very pretty and gorgeous. It was still touching when those same words came from a person I was in love with.

I knew my limits. However, it was always very disgusting when anybody ever tried to force my hand. Some people in high places take women for granted and try to buy their willingness or deal with them with heavy hands.

Today I have turned twenty-seven years old after spending my five years in jail. What good and bad things that have happened in life have disappeared into thin air. What I was; what I did; how I spent my time; who did what and why; and why I was being confined in dreadful jail for no crime at all were things that were knocking some sense into me but not things that could spark my interest in knowing the answers thereto.

What really inspired me during my stay in jail was to

start my life anew. The charms of change had in store many challenges which I was also to face. But I was captivated by the beauty of civilized life which was waiting for me outside the jail as I was not to return back to my rural area.

My father and mother died one after the other during my first three years in jail. I had no sisters and no brothers. This again added a lot to my loneliness and also to my freedom by delinking me from my horrible past.

Everything behind me was reportedly vanished and I was not into repeating all those things with my doll Zuhra – the thought of which had been eating into my vitals. This time, I was not, at all, to dive in headfirst. The things which had done more harm than good in my life were not to be rewound.

# Chapter Thirteen

Yes, I was smitten with love. The story of my love is a story of love that really had no eyes, no mind but only a heart to feel the warmth of someone's personality who fancied me when I started dating with his ideas.

I had grown a chronic reader of the stories of a person who had really pierced the depths of my entity. It was the tale of the afternoons of my term in jail, when I was learning to read and write.

For piquing my interest in reading stories, my tutor had handed over a bundle of his stories. The writer, who I had a crush on, was known by the name Jibraan.

I got the hots for this guy when I came to feel that he knew me and he was the master of gender sensitivities. His write-ups revealed to me that the character he was depicting in his stories was none but me.

One of his stories, which I wanted to share here, was the difference he portrayed between marriage and love. It was the reading of that text that made my heart freeze and it never melted until I came to know that the love as he said is not what you get and what you need but it is what you wish for, you yearn for and what you desire for. I found reflections of myself in his writings.

Jibraan talks through the lead character of the story, who speaks to his friends after losing so much in his love.

He writes:

'What I talk about is not something that necessarily happened to me but is something that happens every day in many lives. Beauty catches people's eye uninvited and unwarranted. Any person of any gender from any part of the planet can fall the happiest victim to this heart-assassinating phenomena any time. No one ever prepares for it nor is anyone prepared for it; it falls accidentally from unexpected corners of life. But when it comes, it comes in style of celebrative and ceremonial march on the grounds of the heart with all pomp and show of human emotions focused on the beautiful beloved. The dancing hearts in such march of love are those which are the victims so bewitched by the beloveds while the rest always stays as silent spectators. It is a shocking show where winning is of less value than racing of hearts.'

This expression of the writer took my helpless heart to the marathon of heart-racing where I was quite in the dark as to whether a person for whom my heart is going to race would himself allow his heart to race in return or just sit on the fence as the viewer.

And very important, whether he would be there or not, to see the dance of my heart and the power of my love for him or whether he really existed ever or was merely a name. To say 'love is blind' is a real not a proverbial expression. It happens in reality.

Keeping in view his killing discourse on love, I was really preparing myself for getting a purpose, so interwoven in my life, to stay focused on doing things for the victims of heart as well as mind equally well. I was planning to be a victim healer.

But I had in my mind a resolve that I would find Jibraan once I got released after completion of my term and to meet him to let him know that I knew him and I had been carrying his torch for the last five years. It all was strange for me. But I had all this purpose for my remaining life.

Jibraan, talking about love and marriage, writes:

'Marriage is what we do by design and by will; while love is what is born and grown unnoticed initially by total default...

Design always pollutes love while default keeps love above board.

Marriage survives and succeeds only in love but love does not depend for its survival on marriage.

Love always has rivals while marriage has many friends on its side. The seat of love is the heart while the chair of marriage is the mind.

Though in some cases marriage can cement love, in many cases it undermines love into a mechanical and formal bond.

Love is innate in human beings and marriage is achieved while in society.

Marriage is rule-bound while love knows no rules, no age limits, no documentary evidence, no material or physical verification. Marriage does all this.

Marriage limits; love frees.

Marriage determines; love liberates.

Marriage is formal; love is informal.

Marriage is social while love is spiritual.

Marriage is lawful; love is divine.

Marriage is a human trait; while love extends to the divine also. Marriage involves sex; love does not necessarily require it. Marriage is primarily a physical bond, while love is essentially an emotional attachment.

Marriage results in offspring, while love turns into a discovery of true humanity and lasting memory.

Marriage is remembered by families while love is remembered by the world.

Marriage is an earthly and worldly institution, while love is power worldly and otherworldly, earthly and celestially.

Marriage is strength, while love is power.

Marriage transforms into progeny while love lives in history as well as in human consciousness.

Therefore, marriages are transitory, while love is eternal.'

Jibraan was right; marriage was no match for love. I had had both experiences. Generally, people fall in love with those whom they marry in the case of a pre-marriage relationship or they start loving when they get hitched.

Marriages can tie social knots but are unworkable in most of the cases in knotting the spiritual ties. As for my two marriages, I always went through bits of rough patches in my marital life. I always remained in blazing rows with my husbands.

Since both were no more, I don't know whether I was fortunate or unfortunate but I was happier than I had ever been during the days of my marital life. I never ever knew before that love was something that is so close to our heart and that the heart is the producer of happiness and truth.

'The heart to me is a bed of God while the mind is a home of the devil. The heart makes us generous and loving while the mind makes us greedy and jealous. The mind to me needs material things while the heart requires emotions as its feed. The mind connects us with this material world while hearts keeps our spiritual link with other worlds', I believe.

The ideas of Jibraan had caught my heart well, yet I knew the dead end of my having a soft spot for him.

I knew it was a pure gamble but I started playing it with the intention of losing it in terms of progressing it into some formal relationship which seemed to be a distant dream to be realized keeping in view my own circumstances.

But I was on it because the cosy feelings gave animation and momentum to the life of my love.

# Chapter Fourteen

During my jail days I learnt how to read and write. After two years I started writing my personal diary. I inserted all important and unique events into my diary to keep a record as to how I spent my days.

Let me share the excerpts of entries in my personal diary. I wrote about the bitter memory of my first day in this way:

'Today it is Tuesday, 2.15 pm in the afternoon, cops, including ladies cops have brought a letter of the court which directs police to hand over our custody to jail authorities. Lady police officer staring at me behind the bars and opening her old purse in very pathetic condition of leather that has lost its face due to scratches of sweat-ridden dirty hands of lady cop, takes out a rolled letter and says to officer in-charge of police station: 'Where is lady accused named Hoor and her children, I have to take them to jail custody now urgently.'

Officer in police station replied: 'Calm down. Have a seat. Take some water. It is too hot outside. Even birds are not opening their eyes due to burning sun. I have taken eight glasses of water in an hour. Please let us complete legal formalities first and you will be signing receipt of accused and will give us in writing.'

On this, Lady Officer got infuriated and reacted in anger telling sarcastically to the officer-in-charge: 'Please don't teach me law. I know my duty. I have to go to home after shifting them and I am badly short of time as very recently I had a child who is an infant and who needs my care but duty is duty Mr. so I request for expeditious delivery.'

Officer replied losing his breath: 'Oh, I understand your problem as I have almost the same problem back home. I have small kids who have no mother, so I look after them; she died in a road accident.'

Lady Constable said: 'I am sorry for her'. Officer responded: 'It is ok.' Their talk was over. Formalities completed. We were handed over.

Lady Constable's name was Raziya. She did not handcuff me as she had very strong sense and experience of dealing with prisoners. She told officer in response to his advice that she should be careful as she is transferring very high profile accused; she said smiling: 'Don't worry, I know my job and I know these accused persons are different; they will not flee away.'

Raziya takes my left hand and crossed her four fingers of her right into my fingers very tightly with crossing her right arm into my left very comfortably. She got us into Suzuki Carry Van with other two male constables.

The van was in a ruined condition with its silencer broken and with its engine crying for repair and releasing too much smoke. We left. Raziya rolled down the windows of both sides as air was dead and everything was just burning. Van was suffocating inside. Raziya was heavy and fleshy, so she was sweating like anything. We had not taken a bath for last fifteen days or so and we were feeling very smelly and stinky, adding fuel to Raziya's fire of discomfort.

But she zipped her lips in anguish. Only looking here and there and asking, time and again, the driver about when he was going to get there. But poor driver was in double dilemma. On the one hand vehicle was not in a condition to dance to his tunes and on the other there was bumper-to-bumper traffic at school time in the metropolis with sizzling heat. After fifty minutes of the worst journey, we reached Karachi Women's Jail where many things were waiting for me.

I got out of the hellish van. It was too hot. We had sweated so that we had become all wet as if we had showered in rain. Jail officers received us in a very rude manner. The Lower ranks used to deal with new arrivals as per practice, while the departures of inmates were dealt with by senior officers. It was a settled tradition of jail because those who were leaving were leaving having washed their sins and guilt while those who were coming were bringing sins and dirt of crime, so proven, needing cleaning. The jail authorities feigned to be the dry cleaners. They pretended to wash not clothes but humans. This was what they presumed about themselves.

So clerks and constables completing the legal formalities welcomed us with sticks and start beating me as if I had arrived in hell and angels were beating me but suddenly it neither came to my mind that angels never beat innocent people nor punished them; these are humans who do so with their fellow creatures.

I requested lady constable to stop beating my kids. She went red-faced in anger and said that she would spare them only on condition of beating me on their behalf. I agreed. My kids were crying and I was also, seeing them that helpless in this world of human beings, who hurt others just for nothing but, perhaps, for entertaining themselves and creating their stories of power and heroism of beating to death or of correction of convicts of crime in whom these officials had no doubt that they were criminals and sinners.

My daughter was bleeding from her left ear due to repeated slapping of that wild lady constable. She kept on beating me on my back like hell. Though she found me deaf and dumb yet not blind because even in extreme pain of stick shots which took away my skin, creating rashes and injuries.

Despite all this torture going on, my eyes focussed on my daughter and also on my son who were weeping and crying for help. But no one was there to hear them and to tell them that everything in their life would soon get better and that there was any hope for them. I was not talking to ruthless lady who was hell-bent on getting us all on our feet. A voice emerged inside my mind to raise a cry for her mercy but I did not because I believed that I had done no wrong, had harmed none, had not killed or kidnapped anyone.

When she got tired of beating me I lost senses and fell on dust in that very hot day. They took me and my kids to hospital there inside the jail for my treatment. It took me four days there to recover.

After I was discharged from hospital, I requested them to allow my daughter to live with me in the women's hall, where I was accommodated. After much pleading they agreed to this with advance notification that she would ultimately have to go to the juvenile section. With the bunch of my clothes, I was languishing to my place in hell, where I was to join thirty other unfortunate lady inmates imprisoned for various heinous crimes. The allegations against me were that of kidnapping and killing which were felonies. Among my hall mates, six inmates were very violent and wanted to subdue me by all means because they were leaders backed by jail administration to keep the inmates disciplined and compliant. Lady Constable who kept on beating me to unconsciousness came and whispered in their ears about my stubbornness. My hall mates went very careful and a little scared. I remained quiet and very calculated in my response to my mates.'

So was the description of my day one in jail. That was the day I faced humiliation. Unforgettable for me were the females, let alone males, who were hell-bent on damaging me to the extent of irreparability. I thought of women who were killed by their men on different ground. Their death saved them from the inhumanity and nasty behaviour of state agents that I had undergone.

# Chapter Fifteen

Going through my own diaries, I just went into the state of mind as to how seven long years ticked in a blink of an eye. Everything around me was the same. The room was the same; the routine was the same; the jail guards were the same; other staff was almost the same; the day was the same; the night was the same; all the days of the week with different names were the same; the faces inside the barracks were almost the same long term.

The only change was the person inside me who was not the same as it was at the time I was brought to the jail. Now this person had become stronger, more patient, more forbearing and more determined.

Now I was changed categorically. I became more confident, more composed, more caring, more daring, bolder, more humane, more understanding and more seasoned.

One day, I had received news that soon I would be set free and would be out of bounds within only a few months. A justice of the high court had committed during his visit that those who had been good and compliant inmates and had followed rules with honesty would be condoned for some years.

My imprisonment was in its eighth year. I had always received good certificates and rewards for my good and positive behaviour inside the jail. So much so that lady constables had become my intimate friends who used to bring for me cloth, shoes, homemade food and many other articles of daily use because I was very personal and cooperative with them.

Since I was not a criminal in the sense of the word nor had I any criminality inside my mind so I never hated cops. I always liked them.

A lady constable had grown to be my close friend. Her name was Maheen. She used to put make-up on me and was always eager to set and dress my hair as she claimed to have worked at some beauty parlour before joining the police force. She always told me that I was very beautiful, no less than a film star or model.

On first seeing me, Maheen always used to say this sentence with a prominent smile on her face, 'Oh, here is my queen, my star, my heroine, my model and my idol, whose worth and depth the world is yet to know.'

Though a very soothing sentence as a matter of fact, yet it made me laugh. My being like a model was perhaps an illusion, which she had because she liked me. So she used to ignore my faults. Only I knew what had happened with me and how I had been protecting my chastity.

No one except me could feel the pain of leading a life without choice and the pain of being forcibly loved and married by someone whom I neither ever knew before nor yet ever liked.

This state of consciousness took me to losing myself, damaging my ego, subjugating my conscience, and conquering my mind and my whole existence, not by feeling humans but by human robots that were often free and immune from what was emotional and what was personal.

A solitary journey of lonely existence had all along been very killing for me. I, I, and I are what I really have been! One day, I was revisiting my jail diary I found some very interesting pages, which I want to share here.

Page 207 Saturday 21 May.
'It was an hour before dawn. I was feeling severe pain in my abdomen. Light and darkness were rolling on my consciousness. I felt my time was counted; nothing worked properly. I was trying to cry for help but my tongue did not receive my command nor did any of my techniques work. What I did then to invite the attention of my roommates was hit my glass bangles, which created a very ugly and irritating noise.

Sanam, an inmate sleeping near me, woke up and began to see my strange body movement. She got closer, trying to make an idea as what was actually going on with me and my body. I am thinking why she is so sceptical and why does she not check me. She does not check until I lost my patience and cried like anything. She brought water for me. She got other mates up but except for the guard there was no one there to attend us and do something urgently to arrange some doctor or ambulance.

Finally after three hours of killing pain, I was in a clinic for treatment. A doctor named Amjad said I was already very weak and that night I had eaten some stale food, which was poisonous. I had severe food poisoning.

On hearing the doctor's comments, prison staff went out of their wits and started shits for all, including me. They blamed me as a pretender as all others were well who ate the same food. Doctor were at their throats, asking them why they were as defensive as he had not declared their kitchen's food as poisonous but rather he had said the patient (I) was suffering from food poisoning.

Doctor Amjad said to the jail staff, 'Since your kitchen is not inside the belly of the patient nor has the patient necessarily been affected by your kitchen's food. I have said what the patient's diagnosis suggests to me and I can't say what you are telling me; nor could you educate me in my job. You do your job and I am doing my job.'

'What you really need to do', said the doctor 'is to worry about your innocent and helpless inmates who have none of their relatives in jail. The government pays you for keeping them safe, sound and healthy.'

'Jails are not made,' the doctor further illustrated, 'to make people ill nor yet to kill them but to restore them, revive them, resuscitate them, rehabilitate them and correct them if they have genuinely fallen victim to any wrongdoing of anyone or have themselves wronged others; I believe and have studied that more than 60% of inmates who are sent to jail are whiter than white and are victimized by our own follies.'

The doctor was unstoppable. He continued, 'Instead we keep already innocent aggrieved persons as guilty, we convert jails into hells for them. As a result, these innocent and pure souls develop anarchical mindsets, losing all belief in the state and its laws which such aggrieved and victimized souls take as draconian and devilish.'

The doctor opened all barrels of remarks by going very predictive and judgemental in saying, 'If we fail to send them back safe, sound, healthy and happy, they will not allow us and our children to stay safe, sound, healthy and happy outside the jail when they are out. They will become criminals for revenge, not for hunger and poverty.'

The doctor quoted his teacher who taught him a lesson, 'If you want to judge the discipline and order of a nation, just observe their traffic and their culture of following rules

90

therein,' shared the doctor, 'and if you want to gauge their humanity, just see how they deal with their vulnerable groups, people with disabilities, people imprisoned, elderly people, sick children and women.'

'This will reflect the power of their civilization and will unfold the strength of their society,' so advised the doctor to jail staff.

Doctor Amjad finally pricked their conscience with the words: 'Here we are dealing with a woman who appears very innocent to me. I believe she must not have been involved in what she has been imprisoned for. So deal with her conscientiously.'

Hearing the doctor's passionate advice, I stood fully treated because I wanted to say some words to the jail staff but I could not find a suitable opportunity to speak my heart I was happy knowing that though we had been confronting bad guys throughout our lives, there were really exceptional characters and minds who take everybody's matter as their own personal matter and who consider their nation as their own family.

Despite odds in jail and the fact that I was jailed for no crime, I took my imprisonment as my boarding school where I had learnt a lot that I would never ever have been able to do outside in the society, which stored many problems and challenges for helpless and homeless people like me.

# Chapter Sixteen

Creativity in ideas and emotions is the garden of guidance and the beauty of human life. There is a lot in life to know and to feel. There are very remarkable things to observe and there are very noble souls to be understood, I believe.

The solitude exposed amazing things to me. It was perhaps the ideal time to delve into self and to know its depths and heights. And the education in the world, till time immemorial, established the fact that understanding self is door to knowledge.

Self study is whole study, the right study, the ultimate study, and the true study because in understanding self, I understand myself and my true person who in turn reveals me who is for me and who is not, I have learnt.

Self image also guides as to which trail I have to tread in life. Nothing ever offered me any opportunity to understand myself better than the solitude which I co-existed with for the last almost eight years.

My inner person always reckoned: my freedom chained, my liberty absconded, my love is still to grow and my world-view is yet to attain soundness and maturity. It was only my solitude which filled the gap of my other missing half.

Here I would reproduce some of the reflections of my life and love from my diary.

Friday, 10pm, Page 150.

'I am half. I don't know what to do with my loneliness. How can I find some emotional support? There is no one to reckon with, and no one to find at my frequency. I feel I overstay here in this world; I am no more relevant. It is my solitude and only my solitude which accompanies me in the dreadful darkness which blurs my foresight and which overshadows my hope of revival to a life which attains its meaning with a man who is yet to think of me, to find me, to know me, to understand me, to like me, and to love me.

But I, on my side, have encircled the name of a man who I feel strongly about, who I have not seen, who I have not talked to, who I really don't know, who I don't know what to do with and who, I know, is the first and the last man on earth to break the locks of my love without making any effort about it. I don't know how old he is; how good he is; how charming he is; how friendly he is; how noble he is; how romantic he is; how fanciful he is; how loving and caring he is; and how meaningful he is! I really don't know how civilized he is! The person like me, who are lost somewhere in the injustices of the system and culture, can only entertain a hope for the best, nothing less nothing more.'

I knew very little about him. He was a prolific story-writer. As I already mentioned about Jibraan, his ideas and views captivated me beyond measure and his interview about his personal life was another boost to my feelings about him. Let me share and reproduce his interview with a journalist, Mr Raheel, of the local paper. The interview script goes as follows:

Raheel said in a very jubilant mood: 'Mr. Jibraan. It is great pleasure to have you in my programme, *Knowing Thyself,* a series interviewing prominent and outstanding figures in their fields.

Jibraan started his opening in the programme 'I feel honoured having been invited on such a prestigious forum.'

Raheel came very curiously, revealing: 'I have many questions to ask and our viewers are anxious to know a lot more about you as you have a large fan following.'

Jibraan consented in a very composed stature, 'Yes, sure.'

Raheel requested Jibraan, 'Please introduce you as many of us do not know about your private life and background.'

Jibraan took a long breath and began his introduction.

'Well, I am Jibraan Khan from Karachi. I am the son of Zamran Khan originally from Hyderabad, Pakistan, who had been in the armed forces on the civilian side and who retired prematurely due to his disability caused by a bomb blast in the cantonment. He is in his seventies.'

Coming to himself, he said.

'I am the only son of my parents and live with my parents, father Zamran and mother ZarGul, in my father's house. My schooling has remained very humble in government schools. I have always topped Board and university exams. I have graduated in English literature and post-graduated in mass communication. I am presently working for a national English newspaper, *The Voice of the People* as a story-writer and editor of its fiction section titled: *My Vision, My Fiction*.

Raheel again indicated his curiosity regarding Jibraan's main characters in his stories being the females with these words:

'Yes, your story-writing skills are marvellous. I also read your stories regularly. In your stories your lead characters are, in most of the cases, women. You always speak through your female characters very comfortably and very powerfully, infusing life to your own feelings and ideas by divulging your very organic thoughts in your revealing words.'

Applauding Jibraan's ways as a writer, Raheel came to his specific question.

'Is there any special reason for it or do you just think that they sell well, so you go for this theme?'

Jibraan, appreciating Raheel's apt question, unveiled: 'Thank you for appreciating my work. It is never like this. I don't select themes. I pick my stories from real world. Finally, I make up my mind to create a character that fits well in my story. I am not a female panellist, nor yet a feminist in any sense.'

Jibraan invited Raheel's attention to his approach as a creative writer:

'I am a free man with a freelance approach. My mind remains in search of real issues. I plant my conscience to locate pain in the society. They both together find the pain in the society that in most of the cases dwells in women's hearts or women's worlds, griping her fortune more disturbingly than any other segment in the society. I explore my themes and characters which bring into life my writings; I am not a type of a writer who follows his pre-decided and pre-listed themes to write for being paid in return.'

Further elaborating the moral roots of his vision and ideas, Jibraan went on putting into words, 'and I write as a passion, wherein I say what I think is right, without any pre-thought of impressing anyone or with intent of hurting someone. I have no target audience in my mind. I have pain inside me for all those who are in pain for different reasons: some have natural and others have man-made pains.'

Expressing the peace of heart, Jibraan verbalized, 'I feel inner solace to give the voices of the people, who are in pain, and a ventilation to reach the relevant corners worldwide and so that someday could find their healing.'

Raheel glowingly admitted and asked, 'Great. Many modern analysts of modern fiction believe that Jibraan Khan is a new voice in fiction writing, an innovative trend of its own kind. How do you see this observation?'

Jibraan remarked, 'This is not what I say and this is what modern analysis of fiction reveals as you maintain. I believe those who say this can explain this in a better way. What I add here is that I am not a good follower of traditions and conventions in fiction writing nor yet I am over-excited to think big. What I know is that be simple as much as you can and be yourself.'

In a very original and advisory tone Jibraan brought out: 'Speak your own words in your own tone, and your own voice on your own problems of life which you are entrapped into, instead of thinking about idealistic interpretations of life wherein a female labourer in Pakistan is wishing to be the queen of England in fiction and an unlettered person becomes a writer or so on and so forth. What defines me is my own natural and original style in highlighting the genuine and practical issues smouldering around us in our neighbourhoods, in our streets and in our homes.'

Jibraan spilled the beans about the element of possibilities of realities in his themes in these words:

'I always write on something that possibly is, that possibly exists, that possibly happens, that possibly is human and that possibly is social. The reason behind this is the facts that there are lots of issues we are facing that badly need our attention than what we need not to invent and to add into already prevailing long lists of our problems. That's why I prefer to stay what I am instead of struggling to be what I should be.'

Raheel lauded Jibraan, 'Very nice. Your originality and

independence of thought is beaming in your answers and speaks louder than your claims that 'you are you'. Can you tell me about your marital life as I think you are over forty?

Jibraan replied: 'I am single.'

Raheel in utter surprise cross-questioned him, 'There must be some reason for your being still single?'

Jibraan cross-answered him by throwing light on his marital philosophy, 'I don't know exactly but I don't take marriage as a necessary evil. What means more to me is the person who I am going to marry!'

Adding to this Jibraan worded, 'In addition to this, what I mean to a woman, I am to marry, does matter. Who means what to whom is 'something' that would define my going wedded?'

Raheel further tried to narrate concisely what Jibraan wanted to say, 'So you are yet to find someone who means something to you and to whom you mean something. Should I understand it this way?'

Jibraan confirmed him, 'Yes to a great extent, you have perfectly understood it.'

Raheel further asked him, 'Have you ever been proposed to?'

Jibraan affirmed, 'Yes, many times.'

Raheel tried to invite Jibraan's attention towards folklore marital perceptions, 'We have heard from our elders that couples are made in heaven. What is your take?'

Jibraan flashed ambivalence by saying, 'Maybe I am not sure that despite giving humans ability to reason, why this is all necessary to be pre-decided. I have my own take on this point. To me, it is the man or woman who decides but when he/she fails in keeping healthy relations with his/her other half, he/

she complains of misfortune, while if it succeeds he/she boasts credit to his own wisdom and smartness.'

Jibraan exhibited his knowledge of religious teachings in terms of marriage and couples: 'However, my understanding of world religions tells me that God has made human beings a superior creature and has empowered them with intellect and has sent guidance for them to understand and to take decisions for making their life beautiful on mother earth, because He has made human beings responsible beings with knowledge and guidance to do the best for themselves.'

Jibraan further announced what he inferred.

'Therefore, on earth humans have developed marriage, family, community, state, and also humanity as the most favoured institutions. So, it will not be wrong to say that marriages are decided and done here in this world. Many may differ with me; I respect their disagreement.'

Raheel eagerly turned inquisitive to know his criteria for spouse selection, 'Who we should presume would be queen of your heart? Do you have any specific criteria in your mind to share with us: such as beauty, education, family, age, background, race or anything else?' Raheel asked Jibraan.

Jibraan pretended to be mindless in specifying the criteria, 'Words fail me here. No specific criteria in mind but what you have specified certainly none of them. If I forcibly convert the criteria in my mind only two things transpire: Humanity and mutual meaning.'

Raheel felt highly excited having known a unique answer from Jibraan, 'Oh, and blockbuster! Humanity, I can understand; but what does 'mutual meaning' mean?'

Jibraan endeavoured to silence Raheel's inquisitiveness, 'Yes, mutual meaning means the feeling in both the partners that they are not going to wed but they are going to weld their entities into a single existence!'

Raheel was satisfied and understood, 'Got it. It was fantastic, superb, enthralling, indeed. I am just thinking about the power of your words as to how your inner person goes with your astounding ideas and it really dazzles me as to what will be your way of conducting yourself into a relationship which no mediocre and run-of-the-mill woman can afford. Oh man, I really am crazy to know who and where will be your perfect match.'

Raheel, foreseeing the possibilities of Jibraan's soul-mate, re-emphasised, 'Maybe she might be of your own ilk and waiting for you and rejecting proposals, waiting for a man of mutual meaning, which you decidedly are. What I am sure about is the fact that your words and your feelings would find her from among your readers. Isn't it?'

Jibraan very confidently made a point, 'Certainly, I will find her because she lives in me. The distance is her finding me, or her appearing before me physically. I know we will find each other very soon.'

Raheel thanked Jibraan for the interview and wished him the best for his spousal explorations, 'Dear Jibraan, I thank you for giving me time for this interview and hope for the best. Now I know she will find you for sure. Thanks.'

Jibraan was quite unaware that she had really found him. The only distance between me and Jibraan was my bondage. I was in jail and he was on his trail. I never wished his trail to lead him to jail but I dream of getting bail (freedom) to blaze his trail.

# Chapter Seventeen

One day, I went to the office of the jail administration to seek their permission to meet my son and daughter. I had an appointment with the jail superintendent.

When I got into the office on my turn, I saw the jail superintendent (JS) had guests. On my entry both the man and woman turned their faces back and scrolled their eyes from bottom to top, leaving me staggering and a bit embarrassed.

Before I could explain my problem to the jail superintendent, the woman sitting there stood up, turned to me and stepped up to me, stopping at the distance of a one step. I was staring at her in astonishment and she gave me a mild smile and shook hands with me saying:

'Hi, I am Samreen Asad and he is Qadir.'

For a while, I became quite without any expression witnessing new faces and the JS broke the silence saying:

'Hoor, these people work with human rights and a legal aid firm here in Karachi so they want to carry out research work as to why women commit crimes and how they are being restored to normalcy.'

I got her point and her comments broke my seriousness and surprise. I sighed with relief that everything was fine. Samreen said:

'If we could find out that the people are not proven guilty

and are still imprisoned, we will take up such cases to the courts and also the government of Pakistan for instant relief but for all this we will have to come up with reliable evidence.'

On her comment, I mildly commented:

'If you do this you will find many innocent inmates here.'

Samreen raised her eyebrows and put her right hand on my left shoulder staring into my eyes and I into hers, she said:

'I will get all out, if I find all are innocent.'

I responded in applause:

'Yes, you can do this because you are a woman and I understand the power of a woman who can do things in much a better way than a man does. '

She smiled and said:

'I would, for sure.'

Having heard this, I thought I had cheesed her off, perhaps. But the reality was the other way round. She did not mean what I understood due to my own inner insensitivity and insecurity. Samreen was a courageous lady and she wanted to raise my confidence level, and that someone was out there to help the people like me who were in distress due to their helplessness and resourcelessness. However, she knew that there were many who had been put behind bars although they had done no crime. Crushing and squeezing my anguish, I clarified her:

'I never do this nor do I know how to do it. The voice always comes from the heart that allows me no cheating, no pampering, no exaggeration, and no hypocrisy; but rather I say what I feel not what I think I should say merely for point-scoring. So, I really appreciate your intention and work.'

Samreen while leaving and addressing me, said:

'Okay no problem. It's my pleasure. I hope you will join us in our upcoming researchers' group visit to women's jail.'

I assured her, 'I shall make all possible efforts to facilitate your task and myself to get out of prison.'

When she and her companion left, the jail superintendent gave me a bit of a tongue-lashing as not to indulge in arguments with everyone. She very sarcastically said while leaning her face to the right side and her eyes fixed on the roof:

'When will you grow? For God's sake do not consider everyone inmate nor yet a villager! These are very important people and the educated cream of this country.

I replied: 'I am sorry, madam, if it hurts you. I had never intended that I would ever hurt you.'

She stood up straight and took a deep sigh and leaving her chair came to hug me; she said:

'The days of your distress are over and the days of happiness are underway.'

Her comments gave a new life to my determination for making significant headway to my destiny that I had cherished in my mind. I thought at least in this big world of seven billion people, 'There are some people somewhere around us who think about us, about our wellbeing and about our future; though they might surely not be more than merely seven.' I left for my barracks with great hope.

After three days, I read a newspaper in which the news of the government's panel to carry out a research study about why the inmate population of the women's jail is increasing; where the shoe pinches; something somewhere must be wrong within ourselves, our systems or in our society that it produces more criminals than we correct; and also why jails have become nurseries of crime rather than correction. The newspaper read:

Headline:

## 'COMMISSION TO PROBE DEVIANCE IN WOMEN & THEIR REHABILITATION'

'Government constitutes a six-member commission to probe causes of deviance in females and their treatment by criminal justice system. The members of commission include four ladies who are from different fields of life and two males one scholar and other is human rights activist. The details of members are not yet revealed and will be notified soon.'

It further stated:

'The mandate of probe includes:
  What motivates women to commit crimes?
  Why jails are saturated: whether justice system fails to work or there are serious loopholes in grooming?
  How police, investigators, lawyers, attorneys, judges and human rights activists are dealing with women accused as well as victims?
  What jails are doing with female inmates? Are they restoring them or criminalising them?'

This has been the mandate of the commission, which will complete its findings within a year after studying and analysing each case of females who have been convicted in major crimes.

Among thousands of inmates in Karachi women's jail the women with convictions for major crimes were in the hundreds. Among them the genuine committers of crime were not more than 40%. However, I knew full well that more than 60% had not committed the crime for which they had been charged and convicted or sentenced. Only 20% must be those women in jail who had not committed any crime at all in their lives but they got sentences. This step of forming a commission was much appreciated by many circles in society as was evident in new letters section daily and this came as a ray of hope for all inmates who had long waited for someone to come and hear them.

This news brought colour to inmate life. At every corner there were gossips about something good happening; many believed that after a long time at least a hope was born which all prayed to grow into a freedom.

Whispers and smiles on otherwise hopeless faces were something that I felt humans need in their healthy lives; this activity had made the dead come alive in jails and generated the environs of energy, light, hope and celebration.

However, at the very bottom of this celebration were hiding the fears of losing friends who had long lived together. Freedom that was to come, it was to come with parting and dissolution of groups closely attached to one another, who had long been sharing everything seen and unseen under the sun.

While there were still others who were not yet to get any freedom nor were they hoping for it, due to the nature of their cases, but what they were damn sure of was that they were going to lose some of their close companions and friends without getting freedom themselves.

This was even more painful because whatever the case may be the government was not to set all inmates free nor did it mean to do so. Only few genuine cases were destined to catch the eye of the commission for seeking some favours. In a nutshell, what was happening was a very good omen.

Let me come to myself. With the spread of the commission news, all lined up in rows to make calls to their families and were very curious, crazy and beaming in happiness but I was with myself all alone, just thinking who should I call; who should I inform about the good news; who is waiting for us; who will come to receive me when we are set free; who will really be happy and where will I go?

These questions had killed my happiness and I was crying on its corpse.

Freedom from imprisonment, for me and my kids, meant my homelessness, hunger, and vulnerability because I had nothing to do outside as the society and its systems were very ruthless having no room for those who did not matter to its economy.

Here in jail I spent the best part of my life and I had very good memories with walls, paths, trees, its small lawn, and its staff that were like a family or community. That was a home, a community, and a family. And that was the address where my solitude was at its best.

I wrote about my probable freedom after having all the concerns as I have stated in above lines.

Wednesday, 5:20pm, Page 645.
'Amid all the fears of losing friends and a way of life, I will be more than happy if I am set free. No matter if there is no one to come to receive me or welcome me, I will make my own fortune with my own hard pursuits but what I will enjoy are the open breeze, rains, sunlight, the seashores, the rivers, the people and the life that is outside of this big wall and inside are only those who have been rejected to live outside or those who have tried to destroy the beauty of free life outside so are they rendered bereft of living a free life themselves.'

# Chapter Eighteen

It was 11am on Tuesday. I was up and busy learning some lessons from our teacher. A lady constable came and whispered in my ear as she was very frank with me.

She told me, 'A very educated alleged killer woman has entered the jail. She is incandescent with beauty and grace of womanhood but a very defiant lady, mostly about her rights to have every essentials of daily life available on time as if she is the queen of jail send by God to rule us. She bursts all the time. Everyone in our staff just shift her handling to the next official for one reason or another.'

Oh really, so you mean she is beyond your administration's control?' I expressed my surprise.

Lady constable, controlling damage, said: 'Excuse me! Nothing in jail is uncontrollable nor would she be allowed to stay unbridled anymore.'

Again I reiterated my jolt in these words: 'Okay. I know that but am surprised about the wait-and-see policy as it is quite a bolt from the blue for me and unbecoming of a jail staff for being so indifferent to such a stormy lady. However, I don't favour any violence and torture which I have myself been undergoing but since all here get their due so why not she?'

She further disclosed the reasons behind the special treatment of the particular inmate, stating: 'Somebody in our ranks unearthed that she belongs to people in high places in our country, so you know there are some problems with our administration officer's jobs, postings and transfers. Hope you get me.'

On this startling disclosure of lady constable, I said: 'Oh! I see.' I was quite disillusioned.

She further predicted: 'I think our staff would assign you a responsibility to take care of her so that she may not feel lonely.'

I expressed my reluctance in a bit of a sarcastic way: 'Yes, I could be a very good babysitter, but I don't think I could be a good lady-sitter.'

Lady constable further underlining the ground realities maintained: 'May it be the way you wish it to be but, baby, this is jail, not home!'

Responding to her indication, I gave her my take on jail in these words: 'absolutely, this is the jail where miracles can make a crash-landing, I know, and where reasons for doing things with anyone are planted, grown and reaped. I know what happens in jail happens because it is a jail, a social island, asocial, unsocial, anti-social, non-social, out of social, above social, beyond social, near social, ultra social, but not social at all.'

On this she challenged the wisdom behind my presumption, 'So you and I are friends and many women give birth to kids and raise them; how come this is not social? These relationships of people in jail last long because bad timers never forget the time they stay and spend together. I admit jail does not offer family but it does provide a magnetic opportunity to make friendships which last longer than normal friendships. This is what our experience tells us.'

Her advice made me ask her this question: 'Do inmates keep relations within themselves or with jail staff also?'

She responded: 'Hmmm! Mostly inmates themselves.'

My question in queue was: 'Do inmates create enemies here?'

Lady constable answered in the positive: 'Yes, very often.'

Again I cross-questioned her: 'With whom, with inmates themselves or with jail staff?'

She showing the experience said: 'Mostly with jail staff and very rarely with themselves.'

I further concluded her points, 'I sum up the point under discussion in the light of what I had been seeing and observing. Inmates make friends but mostly from within inmates themselves but rarely from within jail staff, while they create enmities but mostly with jail staff and rarely with themselves. Do you see who goes social with whom and why?'

She tried to leave the focus of discussion by stating: 'You see things in depth but I was talking generally.'

I showed her the mirror of what I was thinking about jail life in this way: 'Even if you talk generally, how can a society exist when there are no couples living together; there are no marriages being made; there are no families living together here; there are no organised communities or even groups; there are no social classifications or stratifications; there is, above all, no freedom here to have a choice; and also there is no humanity in these environs which are beaming with segregation, solitude and isolations which avail nothing against the truth of being social!'

Lady constable again tried to divert me having no well-thought out response to points raised by me, she stated: 'My beautiful inmate, for me this jail is my home and I live inside it without any penalty, voluntarily.'

I pressurised her with a logic cloned with apology expressing my inability to understand:

'My dear lady cop, I am sorry if it hurts you, but I am at a loss to buy your so oversimplified logic because:

You are not an inmate; you are not confined;

You don't know the feeling of being confined, even if it be one's own home;

You live with your family; you are paid a salary for living here;

You work here; this is your workplace, not imprisonment for you;

You don't know how it feels when one is away from his or her dearest and nearest ones and the places he or she has lived most of the time – home;

It's not you but your freedom that you feel everything fine even being yourself inside the jail but quite immune from the tension of uncertainty about release and freedom;

You are really unaware of the pain of sharing even your bed, towels, soap, edibles and everything except yourself;

You don't know how it feels when you don't know what is happening with all those family and friends who you love and who you claim can't live without you;

You can't imagine how the clouds of insecurity and vulnerability hover over our innocence and simplicity daily;

Come and live in my place for a week only, you will come to know how a day behaves like months and months act as years. I had seen the free life, the one you have now, where years passed as if they were shorter than the days and hours;

It's beyond your imagination to go through the stigma of being convicted of a crime and then reunited to society which abhors the deviants and resists their re-entry into it after provably running counter to its values and norms.

You might be a mother; I am also a mother;

You can't read my heart as to how it reacts to the state of motherless-ness which is different from childlessness in which mother has borne no child while in the previous case mother has many children but she is not available to her kids;

She fails to offer her children the love, care, and service due to her confinement;

What do you know about the cacophony of radio, TV, mobile phones and many other instruments of communication and information; we live in a disconnected world where you are kept blind, deaf, dumb, and under-informed about what is going on in the world and places where you one day return to!

How can you feel the pains of abuse, you have not committed a crime; you are not convicted and you are not stamped. The tongue of a human being is very lightweight, but only a few know how to carry it and how to bear its weight;

This all happens because these mothers are not at home within their families; they are rather in jails where hardly any law prevails except what the jail administration or staffs, as the case may be, like; their whims and caprices rule supreme.'

Lady constable surrendered with her both hands up, she said: 'Oh my God! Gentle lady I am a tiny worker and earn some pennies to feed myself and my children. I neither make policies nor am I in a position which really matters or where I could make a difference.'

I warned her: 'Again, I am sorry you are badly mistaken. If it is an excuse either to defend you or to avoid argument, then it's very fine. What matters in life, in my opinion, is not your authority or position but your person inside and your thinking. It hardly makes any difference what you can do by virtue of where do you stand but it is sure to make a mark when you try to do a thing that your person inside motivates you to do. You can do a lot more in your capacity. Those who have no job and whose role is not defined nor are they paid for anything, work wonders by self-finding their role. Such souls are called legends that make history forever and ever. I cherish them.'

Lady constable requested for a ceasefire in these words: 'I, with my hands folded, hold my ears; can there be any room for forgiveness in losing a war of words?'

Her body language and style of delivery of words were very annoying for me, so I criticized, expressing: 'You call this merely a war of words and make me feel I am harping on my version of what I feel in jail. It's really very sarcastic.'

My sharp words offended her and she lost all her professional and personal patience by vomiting these words: 'Dear, enough. You are not here to teach me what I should believe and how I should behave.'

I very politely made her understand that we should avoid making sweeping statements about something that has never happened to us. I told her in defence of my point of view: 'Never. I don't mean that. What I am trying to tell you is that we should all have our own viewpoints, complexes and limits. It does not behove any of us to presume moods and state of minds in certain circumstances without having undergone similar situations. You are good at explaining your world and I am better at mine.'

She cooled down saying: 'I can't say anything to you as since the very early days you are on my heart. May Allah save you from anyone's service at which you are very poor?'

I tried to close the track of discussion; I thanked her: 'Just leave it. I am grateful for your timely intimation of what is going to happen with me. I will handle it if the situation so requires me to do as I have been working out evens the worst.'

She realising her mistake, tried to make the environs colourful by saying: 'Ha-ha, this could surely be your unique worst.'

Her comments raised my curiosity to enquire about the new lady inmate; so I asked lady constable: By the way, who is she that is so notorious that even cops are cramping!'

She told me a brief bio of the new powerful inmate: 'A woman aged thirty-five named Rohi is on trial for having killed her own husband. She is a very educated, decent and gorgeous woman. There is a great likelihood of her trial maturing into a death sentence.'

Her brevity did not satisfy my curiosity already raised by her discussions and I went to further ask her: 'Do you know more about her as to why she went to the extent of killing her other half?'

On this too, she gave a one glimpse of the crime for which Rohi was jailed: 'Not many details but the police officials who accompanied her to jail told me overtly that she has a twelve-year-old daughter from her first husband. Her twelve-year-old daughter, named Soniya, was reportedly abused by her second husband, named Samad. She caught him red-handed and killed him with pistol fire in his head. After this I begged leave: 'Thank you very much dear Lady Cop, Maheen, for information. Now, I beg leave as my time is up.'

Lady constable left wishing: 'Dear, has your time; see you. Bye.'

# Chapter Nineteen

A few days later in my barracks, I was thinking of Rohi and the reports about her, which had gone viral in jail those days. Rohi's name was on the lips of every inmate. Everyone was crazy to see her, to meet her, and to establish a friendship with her. I thought, what was so special about her that attracted the rest?

After much thought, I gathered all information about her because inmate ladies had different opinions about her physical appearance, about her education, family background and about her marital relationship. Anyway everyone had her own story and her own version about Rohi to tell. This deepened my curiosity more to personally meet her.

Having that in the back of my mind, I asked some jail staff as to how could I manage to arrange my meeting with Rohi. Maheen, my lady constable friend, advised me to wait as the case of Rohi was a fresh one and many people, detectives, researchers, investigative journalists and many gender-related NGOs were putting tremendous pressure on the jail authorities to allow them a meeting with Rohi for getting their stories ready. She further told me that in such cases nothing matters.

Maheen further educated me:

'One who markets Rohi's story late gains nothing. So this is a cyclonic time for the tycoons of media and ours is a different case.

We plan to approach Rohi once the dust of the storm has settled down completely. Rohi will have time to attend us, to listen to us and to tell us what we are very restless to know about her.'

The jail staff lady was perhaps correct.

After a month, when the wet climate of hot controversies surrounding Rohi's killing of her husband had damped down and the attention of media devitalized, the jail staff lady constable came to me and said: 'Hi Hoor, good afternoon.'

I also wished her: 'Good afternoon, dear. What's up?'

She said: 'Everything is perfect.'

I asked: 'Any news for the commission meeting?'

She updated with no news: 'No update about when, exactly.'

I regretted saying: 'Good news is always rare, while the bad news follows you very honestly.'

She diverted me by disclosing: 'Not that much good news, but I am pleased to tell you that today you are going to meet a like-minded lady, Rohi.'

I expressed excitement: 'Oh really! I can't believe it!'

She was damn definite in her stance: 'You should for sure.'

I said in a happy mood: 'You can see my face glowing and my mood radiating in happiness.'

She confirmed my happiness, which was evident to her: 'Yes, I can read happiness on your face. You look restless to meet Rohi without missing a microsecond.'

I curiously asked the lady constable: 'What have you told Rohi about me?'

She replied: 'Your story.'

I was crazy to enquire as to how much Rohi knew about me: 'My story! I mean to what extent and what have you told her?' I asked very enthusiastically of the lady constable.

She said that Rohi had many details about me: 'I have told her enough details about your life journey and the ordeals you have been facing and an overall picture of how life has been treating you!'

I wanted to know exactly what Rohi was told about me. 'Can you please tell me what exactly you have told her so that I may not miss anything meaningful while communicating with her,' I asked the lady constable in utter amazement.

The lady constable reassured me, 'Sure. I have told Rohi as much as I know about you. Like you, she showed so much interest to know about you.'

Rumours of Rohi's being a crook were afloat and were chilling the ears of inmates. Almost everyone around was overwhelmed by the fantasy of the criminality of Rohi. In all that, I was also carried away by my desire to have an encounter with such a celebrated inmate. Fortune ultimately smiled on me when I was told that the Eid function was being organized in which I, together with some other colleagues, was to perform with Rohi.

This was my news. I was to entertain that news as my passion to have a chance to cultivate a bond with Rohi. I had been hearing a lot about the mysterious circumstances surrounding the murder of her husband as well as her family. Her educational profile was very impressive.

Ultimately, I was to see the dawn that came with lots of new thoughts and new hopes. That day was the day I had to go for rehearsals in a team. At least I was sure about one important thing for me, that I was going to meet a different woman of her own nature and calibre.

And it is eight o'clock in the morning. There is a big hall inside the jail in which a performance stage has been installed.

There are lots of performers waiting and looking for their team members. I was locating my heroine. There was loud whispering of different voices and words crossing through the ears and the air.

My sight fell and just fixed on an awesome lady. My eyes stopped twinkling. Suddenly, a colleague patted me on the shoulder. I had just become a statue. After a while I was revived to the environs.

When I was back to normalcy she scolded me as to where I was lost. In response to her question, I asked her, 'Do you know who that lady is in the white gown?' To my utter wonderment, I came to know that she was the one whom I had been idealising and waiting for. She was our team leader, Rohi.

Rohi appeared to me tall in height, fair in complexion, enthralling in features, bewitching in figure, and very gorgeous in appearance as if she has just landed somewhere from a celestial world – a beauty personified and glorified with undoubtedly a character dignified.

On this, my colleague stared in my eyes and said, 'What is so special about her?' I told her, 'I don't know the speciality in her; what I am really excited about is her hair-raising stories which my consciousness wants me to explore!'

Finishing with her quickly, I went straight to Rohi for saying regards and introducing myself as the team member. The way she smiled in response, the way she hugged, the way she kissed, the way she expressed strong passion and warm gestures of her involvement and attention to an ordinary person like me was, indeed, something that arrested my mind, moved my heart, and romanticised my mood at the instance of my first but curiously awaited interaction with her.

I found that she had all the guts of being a charismatic

personality that she decidedly was. After having an exchange of brief introduction, I asked Rohi to arrange a private meeting with me someday so that I could exchange some personal thoughts with her regarding the problems of female inmates in the jail as well as some personal issues as she reportedly belonged to a very powerful political family and was damn confident about her getting away with all that criminal justice stuff very soon.

Her response was very positive and we were to meet within the next few days. So after rehearsals everyone was back to their places. That day I felt some sort of consolation and extrication that Rohi could be of some help to me at least when I completed my term here or could get me out through legal and human rights help even before.

# Chapter Twenty

After three days we met in her room in jail. She was not living with any other inmates. She was alone. I asked her as to how the jail administration kept her in the political inmates' section since she was accused in a murder case.

In response to my question, she smilingly said: 'Where are you lost sister, this is city of Karachi. Here everything has a price and here every official is either purchased or sacked or even eliminated in case of their denial to oblige and to give favours; Power does matter here.'

She further enumerated her claim.

'All here are very good with me. The reason behind my arrest as well as prosecution is our unbridled media, which was hell-bent on campaigning against me due to some political underpinnings. Otherwise no First Information Report (FIR) or a police case of murder of my husband would have been lodged at police station. We had all the arrangements to get this murder declared as a suicide.'

On her observations and understanding of the system, I was taken aback. I was lost in deep thought rewinding as to what had happened to me since I had neither killed nor kidnapped anyone but rather was myself fallen easy prey to the forced marriage cult in our male-dominated society. She, too, was silent then and her jaw dropped on my response of non-response.

Being uncontrolled by curiosity which killed her hesitation as it did in my case to see her, she tried to bring me back to real time by asking me a question as to why I was being kept in jail and for how long.

I responded, 'I was innocent; I had committed no crime at all. I was detained and punished for the crimes of those who had committed crimes against me and my very existence.'

She in apparent shock pressed me to share details of my case with her.

I narrated the whole story of my going behind bars and getting a sentence in the court of law in these words: 'I was forcibly married at the age of ten to an unknown person who was more than eighteen years older than I was at the time of our marriage. When I was eighteen and had had two kids, one girl and one boy, my husband was killed by a notorious criminal who forcibly married me and kept me with his existing two wives as his third wife in his hideout in the dense jungles of the Indus River in upper Sindh where he had established a camp of criminals and where he used to keep kidnapped persons for making ransom deals.'

Further recalling my bad old days, I continued to narrate.

'I had no other option but to manage to get rid of all this. For having all this in mind, I came in contact with a cop who I found keen and capable of helping me, which he did to a great extent.'

Giving more input, I admitted, 'I got rid of that criminal husband, as he was shot dead in an encounter with police while he, along with me and my kids, was trying to transport a foreigner hostage from one place to another, using me and my kids as a human shield and as a camouflage to put dust in the eyes of cops, pretending that he was a gentlemen and that he was travelling with family.'

I also confessed to Rohi that I got my criminal husband, who had forcibly married me by rendering me a widow and my kid's orphans, eliminated by giving full information to the chief cop who promised to take action against him. I continued with mixed feelings.

'His (Meeral's) pretentions on his part, but police knew full well as to what he was and with whom he was travelling and why. Police recovered the hostage and on his statement booked me and my kids in a criminal case for allegedly kidnapping and killing many people as gang members. Even my kids were incriminated as facilitators. We were being punished for the crimes of Meeral who was a notorious dacoit.'

I repented in penitence.

'The court sentenced me to ten years in jail. I came here with my kids as they had no one outside and I was very scared to run the risk of keeping them away at the mercy of cruel society especially my daughter, Zuhra. Besides this, they both were too young and there was no one to financially and emotionally take care of them. Here they remained in safe custody though I was never safe here.'

In grave anguish, she said, 'I did not know what had happened to you could possibly be happening to someone else in our society – very unfortunate, indeed.' Rohi, hugging me, said that I was the perfect case of grave victimization of the systems of all kinds in our country and in our society.

She further deplored with rue.

'My hair has been raised hearing your story of a continuous punishment for being innocent all the way. First your family and father, then a criminal, then the police, then prosecutors, then the courts, none could read or could bother to see your innocence that was so clearly branching in your entity at all levels of your life. Rather, on the contrary, almost all who had a physical interaction with you kept an evil eye on your chastity and integrity and left no stone unturned to abuse or molest you.'

Without stopping, she exalted my forbearances.

'And you being a weaker vessel kept on bearing all this stuff considering it your destiny and kept on falling victim to nasty compromises to survive. I have a firm belief that God must have a reward for your patience and forbearance in both the worlds and the world we live in must know about your celebrated character to stand the crises of womanhood in our society. I promise you, I will let the world know your struggle for your being in our society.'

When I asked Rohi about the truth of the murder case she was alleged in, she, taking a long breath, said 'Our cases have resemblances; you got rid of your husband by providing information to the police in good faith while your first husband was killed by your second husband and so you avenged the death of your first husband. Similarly, I got rid of my second husband to avenge the molestation of my daughter at his hands, while the father of my daughter and my first husband died of a heart attack some years back.'

Without any compunction, she confessed her crime.

'I don't deny having killed him but any mother would have done this and I have no regrets for it. I have honour-killed him as he played havoc with my trust. So, I deserve and have claimed judicial relief. I will do the same for you to prove you innocent.'

# Chapter Twenty-One

A few days later, the commission had started its work of fact finding. On my turn, I appeared before the commission members and presented my entire case of innocence and they assured me for belated justice. After thorough perusal of the cases and detailed interviews with inmates, the commission recorded the facts and made their finding public after one month.

### EXCERPTS FROM COMMISSION FINDINGS

We have, on the direction of human rights ministry, examined the six hundred cases of women accused, detained, and sentenced with mandate of exploring the merit, police handling, fair trial, fair treatment of female inmates and also victimization so caused at any stage of law enforcement and prosecution processes.

To anyone's utter surprise, we have only been able to declare 30% cases fairly dealt with and only 2% cases were found genuine while 98% cases were found to involve false implications in which 28% were dealt with well, though being false. In our findings only 2% of female inmates had actually committed the crime they were detained for while the rest were non-committers, either those who were totally innocent, who knew who had actually committed the crime, and those who abated crime. Overall we found more than 60% of female inmates innocent with strange stories and heartrending truths.

We must share one leading story of Hoor who was sentenced for a ten-year term and who was innocent beyond any doubt. Her story is a big question mark on our system of justice on which we are spending a handsome amount with intent to punish criminality for ensuring order, not to punish innocence to cause anarchy in society. Our society faces unrest because impunity of criminals has become its inherent feature while innocent people face severe sentences. The case of Hoor involves an innocent lady who was detained for crimes she never committed. This commission has taken her story as a case study.

Hoor, a thirty-year-old lady, having two kids, got imprisoned eight years back because of allegedly kidnapping a foreigner. While the facts of her case reveal that she never did that nor was any evidence of her criminal involvement in that kidnapping proved but rather the hostage's release became possible due to her cooperation with the police. Had she been involved, she would never have informed the police at the peril of losing her husband, even if he was a criminal.

Evidence has been put on record through CDRs and statements of the police officers, including then district police officer Ghotki, Mr. Shah Haq, who carried out the operation of recovering the hostage, Tommy Jack, a UN employee, and of eliminating one of the most notorious criminals of all times, Meeral, who carried two million Pakistan Rupees reward money on his arrest, dead or alive. DPO Shah Haq admits Hoor as his lead informer in achieving a success, which would not have been possible without loss, if Hoor had not helped the police. As a professional, Shah Haq also lamented his failure to save Hoor and her family due to his sudden transfer to some other station where, too, he was tasked to fight terrorism.

Besides her false criminalization at the hands of the police investigation, establishing guilt in the court of law and her ten years imprisonment, her own family and society played hell with this innocent soul in the sense of forcibly getting her married long before she was born as she claimed: 'I was wedded before I had seen the world,' and depriving her of husbands thereafter. It appears that she was punished for the sins of others: first she was paid as compensation when she was not even born for the sins of her father; second her so-called husband was treacherously killed by a criminal with the intention of marrying her at gunpoint; thirdly the profession of a person who forcibly kidnapped and married Hoor was kidnapping for ransom and she had not much power to defy his criminal majazi Khuda (worldly king) husband. Neither had she ever wanted that criminal to commit crime nor did she ever participate in criminal activity nor did she ever abate any crime. Just being tied in a forcible marriage bond with rascal Meeral does not entitle her to be sentenced as a criminal convict. Action without motive does not qualify to be described as crime even if it may be very severe or violent whatsoever. Hoor was wedded to Waqar by pure chance; she had never made a choice for it. Similarly, she fell in Meeral's trap by pure default; she never ever did that by design. Therefore, in Hoor's case, motive or intention of crime and criminality is seriously lacking, so her sentence makes her a victim of justice in addition to her suffering in the throes of the system.

Therefore, giving her such a severe sentence speaks volumes about the inefficiency as well as inhumanity of our criminal justice system.

# FINDINGS & OBSERVATIONS OF THE COMMISSION

Victimization of the woman in Pakistan has emerged as one of the leading problems of our systems of the society as well as of the state. Very sadly, our criminal justice system offers a very hostile environment for remedies of gender issues. 'I was wedded before I had seen the world', is not merely a statement of fact, nor only a claim of a female victimization of forcible marriage but it is also a charge-sheet against the weaknesses and discriminations of our criminal justice system to offer a required protection to females against highhandedness of male members, against falling victim to traditions of culture, against the greed of the legal community, and against coercive authority of the state.

The story of Hoor clearly reveals the massive victimization of the woman in Pakistan. It also paints a horrible picture wherein it is shown with alarming clarity as to how the tradition of honour killing plays hell with the innocent lives of both the dead and survivors and as to how private and parallel justice systems take away the fundamental rights of the people in general and that of the woman in particular. It also throws enough light on the indifference of our governmental system that leaves the weaker vessel at the mercy of the cruel decisions of the sardar sand waderas (Local Notables) as well as the brokers of our criminal justice system.

We members of this commission are in complete accord that the womenfolk seem to be the victim of inscribed slavery, imposed hardships, veiled lifestyle, and engineered silence in our country. This phenomenon sends clear signals to every conscientious person to believe that the victimization of the woman in Pakistan is, indeed, a sad tale of culture and system.

It goes without saying that the violence and discriminations against the woman are commonplace in our society. The woman faces massive resistance for everything. If it is the matter of property, honour, or personal animosity of different tribes or people, the woman serves as the best scapegoat for them to settle their scores. Countless women suffer from domestic violence, parental pressures, spousal abuse, forced marriages, unjustified divorces, sexual assaults, burning acid attacks, mutilation, rape and battery.

A very painstaking aspect of this practice is its misuse; most of the women are killed for reasons other than pure honour (as per local narratives of honour) but such killings are regrettably tagged as honour killings. Still more heart-sickening is the fact that the killers of such innocent women are none but their own nearest and dearest ones: parents, siblings, and in-laws. Such innocent women are killed even when the males, against their consent, forcibly molest them. They kill and feel proud as if they are the conquerors of Constantinople. Even the other women do not feel any regret on the innocent killing of their fellows but rather like their males and in some cases even more than them feel honoured and take pride in such inhuman acts of their males. Women like Hoor have a different mindset and they differ from the rest in their approach to life and their culture so have much more tendency to suffer at the hands of hostile systems.

In some cases, it has also been witnessed that mothers have killed their daughters with their own hands. So much so that some women die in disappointment and others kill themselves in utter despair when they see their death approaching due to false allegations. This practice is in vogue mostly in the lower strata of our society and is rarely found in upper and middle classes. Honour killings are, therefore, a sign of pure ignorance and barbarism and tell a crude tale of the helplessness of the women in Pakistan.

If there is anything more disturbing than prevalence of these crimes against women, it is, indeed, the impunity with which such crimes are committed. Our criminal justice system can hardly claim to have offered any reasonable and satisfactory relief package for women victims. It is perhaps the reason why human rights organizations call our criminal justice system 'indifferent at the best' towards the redressal of genuine grievances of women victims. Rather, it harasses and haunts them.

Many social activists believe that it is only because of the rampant incompetence, corruption, biases, unresponsiveness, and hostility of the various actors of the criminal justice system that the molesters, attackers and indeed killers of women go unpunished. When an aggrieved woman approaches police, prosecutors, judges, and media-men for redressing her grievances she faces their lukewarm attitude and she more likely finds further victimization and abuse.

Our findings highlight that a grossly inadequate and discriminatory legal framework is only one of the whole series of hurdles for victims; seeking redress for victims also has to contend with biased officials and outright harassment at every step of the law-enforcement process, from the initial registering of a complaint to the trial. Only the most persistent and resourceful complainants succeed in manoeuvring such hostile terrain, and even those who do seldom see their attackers punished.

The suspects of only two percent of cases of women being killed and molested are reportedly taken into custody and hardly any are brought to justice in the real sense; we have noticed a number of vulnerabilities in women victims and also in all the tiers of our criminal justice system: police, medico-legal doctors, prosecutors, judges, and the prison officers.

## 1. POLICE

Take the example of the police. All the women victims of sexual abuse, acid burning and domestic violence mostly first contact a police station, the '15' helpline or in rare cases a newspaper office. Generally, it's the police that come first but unfortunately the police have lost the trust of women victims as a reliable institution to provide them necessary shelter and security and to redress their genuine grievances.

Sometimes, it really staggers one's imagination that when victims of sexual abuse or domestic violence resort to a police station for the registration of their complaints she encounters a long series of obstacles. It has generally been observed that the police very often misreport their story with a view to create tailor-made weaknesses in their case, and to carve out any easy way for the smooth escape of the culprit from the grip of law and justice. In cases of domestic violence the police avoid them by saying that it is not a police matter but a private one in which the police are not empowered by law to interfere on their own.

Additionally, it has been noticed with grave concern that police widely disbelieve the women and they argue that most of women complainants come with self-inflicted wounds and with concocted stories against their male rivals with a view to blackmail, to pressurize, and in some cases to settle their old scores with them. Sometimes, some mischief-makers purely plant them in order to grind their own axe. However, this is not true always. So, we advise that police must learn to differentiate as to who is right and who is wrong.

## 2. MEDICO-LEGAL DOCTORS

After police come medico-legal doctors. If collected and analysed properly the medico-legal evidence plays a telling role in securing the convictions in the cases of domestic and sexual assaults.

But ironically serious failings do exist in this area also. In many cases the police delay giving official referrals required for the purpose of such examination of women victims in the cases of rape and injury. However, it is in the nature of forensic evidence that it is transient and it is easily lost if timely examination of the victim is not made which is essential and crucial for exonerating the victim from charges of consensual illicit sex. Doctors conduct medico-legal examination in a very haphazard manner, which definitely fails to secure meaningful evidence. Doctors take it not in a serious way and focus mainly on determining whether and when the hymen was broken instead of conducting a thorough analysis of the extent of the severity of the victim's injuries, thereby successfully identifying the actual offender. The virginity status formula badly fails in the cases of married women victims. The doctors, like police, mostly disbelieve the women victims. Medico-legal doctors must now mend their ways and treat women victims very fairly.

## 3. TRIAL COURTS

Almost the same is the case with the court environment. During the proceedings, the prosecutors who are supposed to show all possible sympathies with the victim ask very unethical and indecent questions and hence tamper with the sensitivities of the victim without an iota of remorse. Words like past sexual history of the victim, virginity status, character of the victim, consensual illicit sex etc. are very openly coined in the courts both by the defence counsel as well as the prosecutor about the women that reach the courts for relief and justice. when women victims of violence resort to the judicial system for redress, they are more likely to find further abuse and victimization. The possibility of prosecuting, especially in a context where women victims of sexual violence are routinely disrespected by the state officials, serves strongly to inhibit victims from pressing charges. Judge allows defence council free rein to introduce inflammatory evidence and to attack the victim's character and prior sexual history even when this is patently irrelevant. Therefore, her experience with the judicial system is often more likely to compound the trauma of the original assault than to provide the satisfactions of seeing justice done. We agree with his observations and suggest the law ministry should make arrangements for a safe environment for fair trials without unnecessarily using words and phrases which hurt women or assassinate their character.

## 4. JAILS

Still more awful are the conditions of women in the women's jails in our country. Take the example of the women's prison in Karachi where female prisoners are pooled beyond its capacity. Those women prisoners who are convicted or are on trial for drug trafficking, zina (adultery), kidnapping, murder, robbery and other offences lead a very pathetic life inside the prisons. Hardly any satisfactory arrangement is made for them and their dependent children, especially young girls who are sent to the jails with their accused and convicted mothers. Most of such women prisoners hail from lower-income families. Such mothers have no other option but to keep their children with them in the prisons. Thus, such children, who are enchained for the sins of others, are brought up in an environment that is hostile to the delicacies and sensitivities of infancy and childhood, these unfortunate innocent souls fall easy prey to the haunting environment of hostile motherhood, broken home, segregated community system and apathetic government machinery. Moreover, the personality development of such neglected and uncared-for children shows no signs of improving. Rather, the personalities of many children get crushed in the ugly prison culture of corruption, indifference, neglect and victimization. Hence the women in jails suffer in a variety of ways and they are yet to receive a humane and patient hearing.

## CONCLUSIVE REMARKS

In the backdrop of the prevalence of deep-laid gender discrimination, biases and injustices in our state's justice delivery system, it is, therefore, high time for media, government, non-government organizations, (NGOs) and also the international community/organizations to pool the sum of their wisdom to reason out a 'relief package' for the women victims of diversified crimes, which have taken deep roots in our society and which grow unhindered because of the weaknesses, vulnerabilities and misunderstanding of our culture, law and religion. Government must make a principled decision to set free all innocent female inmates and compensate those who spent their years in jail for not committing any crime.

In order to rationalize things on the ground, our leading suggestion for the government is to take a serious decision on releasing those who are detained for no crime at all. An announcement of Aam Maafi – a general pardon – may see the light of day as this will go a long way in healing the wounds of innocent inmates who await the arrival of a messiah to get them justice and take them out of jail which is tantamount to hell for them.

# Chapter Twenty-Two

I meet Rohi again in her room to tell her about the development of the commission. This time, we had a pretty good idea about each other and this time, our moods were more relaxed in comparison to our earlier meeting's tense environment. From sharing torments to disclosing our romance, we explored our real ladies inside with their conviction in love being the true beauty of life.

Rohi asked me as to whether any man had ever appealed to me? I was very frank to say: yes.

To that she responded at sky-rocketing speed, 'Oh really, I hope you are not kidding with me.'

I made my point clear in these words, 'It is something genuine and not a joke. Equally true is the fact that I have not seen him face to face. I don't know about his personal life. What I know about him is that he is a very accomplished writer and a great feminist.'

'Could you share his name?' Rohi asked.

'His name is Jibraan; he writes stories of women in *The Karachi Times* magazine,' I revealed.

'My queen, you are in love with Jabe; he has been my classmate and good friend for about eight years as we did our university together,' Rohi claimed.

'Great, you must know a lot about him,' I made a fair-and-square admission.

'Sure, he is a man of his own type without having a woman of any type in his life, I don't know why but he has been a very good friend and a nice human being; now I and Jibraan could help you in the light of the report submitted by the commission,' Rohi admitted.

'I don't know much about him nor yet are his details my concerns,' I expressed.

'I am carried away by the way he thinks about us and our woes,' I pointed out.

Rohi very jubilantly and passionately assured me: 'I will catch Jabe once I am out of jail and then I will get you, too, out of jail.'

We were finished with our meeting. I went back to my place in jail.

My meeting with Rohi left me thinking. I realized that the world we live in is a very small place. A character and a person, Jibraan, who is a famous writer and feminist of our country and who I came to know reading his stories, was a distant dream for a woman like me to know about his personal life and his background or to ever think of having any chance to see him; I didn't know how my ray of hope for this had shown up today.

However, I was not at all turned happy-go-lucky because everything in the phenomena called life was almost unpredictable at least for me who never knew nor felt in advance as to how destiny would treat my wishes so well. So, instead of getting very much excited on this chance, I just left it to the 'time and tide'.

Exactly six months after Rohi got imprisoned, Rohi got a release order. No sooner did the news of her release come to me, then I requested our warden to allow me to bid farewell to her. He did and I got the chance to go and see her. Since she was packing up and waiting for some family members to take her home, she was not meeting anyone. But she did not resist meeting me as we had become good friends.

Rohi told me we had only thirty to forty minutes to finish. I had lots of things to share with her but time was very short and the moment was not toned for sorrows. I told her a few things about her offer of what she could do to help me out.

In utter despair, I requested Rohi: 'I need you not to forget that I am a woman; I am alone in the world which houses millions of people. My being a woman is by my destiny but my being a victim is by the system. My destiny is divine but my system is man-made or my own. My case of my destiny I will fight myself, but I need some help for my case of system which is designed to destroy me and my innocence.'

I further expounded heavy-heartedly to Rohi: 'However, my victimization in the system has been convincing me to explore my own hidden powers of patience, tolerance, and forbearance which may not pay me here but I am damn sure they will pay me one day. My belief in my innocence will someday win the day for me.'

I also got the system across.

'The system keeps killing me. Everyone is happy under the spell of the system. My parents sacrificed me for settling their own issues born out of their ignorance, first my in-laws always considered me the 'enemy's daughter' where helplessness and hatred remained my companions.'

I spelled out the tragedies with my womanhood while living in the damn system.

'My second husband used me just for lust and kept me at gunpoint to live a life of siege under his armed militia. The government's criminal justice system did not hear me at any stage nor yet is designed to trust and respect my being already a victim of culture and society. I don't remember that I was ever a non-conformist either of cultural values or of statutory laws yet I fell their worst victim and am now squandering behind bars for no sin or for no crime at all.'

I began to narrate story of my tragedies. 'The circumstances I was in or I inherited were not of my own choice but I was made to live in them by brute force of outlaws; in the same fashion I am detained by the civilized authorities of law. My heart keeps bleeding on my being a woman which seems to be the biggest of all my weaknesses, greatest of all sins, gravest of all crimes and worst of all vulnerabilities.'

Finally, I unfolded myself and the powers innate in women.

'And I live to see all "superlatives" converted into the noblest of all human powers – the power of being a woman, the power of being a daughter, the power of being a sister, the power of being a mother, the power of being a lover, and also the power of being a beloved.'

In a state of heartbreak, Rohi commented: 'We being women do our best to add strong emotional feeling to our all relations and try to stay loyal to them but almost all the way we suffer worst betrayals and illusions throughout our life journey without any repair and without any stop. No one can understand the pain of being betrayed by our own soul-mates and no medical science or psychological study could offer us solutions to our woes except our own selves and our own culture which is broadcast with male dominance and monopoly.'

With wet eyes and with crying hearts, we hugged and departed for that time to meet again on some meaningful forum. A few hours later, Rohi was no longer with us and had attained freedom.

# Chapter Twenty-Three

Rohi took action by taking my case as a model case to challenge and to identify the loopholes and drawbacks in the criminal justice system, which was apparently designed to catch the innocent and to set culprits free. My story made headlines and many experts discussed my case on both electronic as well as print media very extensively.

Rohi involved human rights activists, investigative journalists, voluntary legal-aid groups and non-governmental agencies. The human rights agencies were sensitized for rehabilitation of convicts to address my case with full vigour.

All my details were obtained. My past, my marriages, my kids, my places where I once lived, my investigators, lawyers, a few local journalists who covered my arrest and myself came in focus. Many journalists and legal-aid workers came to meet me in jail.

Some came for unearthing facts while others for enjoyment. For one or the other reason, I was surrounded and the world was gathered around me on my story. As Rohi had advised me to express myself to the utmost for seeking attention and favour, I bared my heart to everyone interested to know my story.

In my frank revelations, I never covered my tracks as I stood 'whiter than white' in my whole conduct so I never bothered. Nor did I ever fear anything. Keeping facts under wraps had not paid me anything. However, some out-of-the-box questions drove me to go beside myself with annoyance, yet I tried to maintain my balance.

Being cut-to-the-quick, I did not have long to wait and in a week or so I was to be released. When good news of my release order reached, a wave of cool breeze touched me and I became very happy. I felt very nostalgic right at that moment. Those were the unique feelings, which I had never experienced before in my whole life.

The walls of jails which always denied me my freedom, the inmates who always shared their sorrows, the jail staff who always pleaded for *majbori* or helplessness to help, all the haunting pathways and everything appeared to me as great physical and emotional protections. Now I was leaving I was feeling like the loser; I was losing, and I was departing. Frankly, the soul was departing from my body.

Actually ambivalence, I must admit, governed me that day. I thought being inside jail was much better than the outside world, where life was more vulnerable and more exposed to a much wider audience and a more insecure environment. Change, which was giving pains apparently, was accompanying inner peace, and solace.

Freedom was free outside jail and everything free always hosts insecurities of different types. However, inside jail too, though freedom chained yet insecurities of its own nature always hovered on inmates. The actions with impunity by jail staff knew no limits and no restraint, which always kept inmates in a state of utter retreat and absolute unsafety. Therefore, I was happy with my freedom as a whole.

It was 10am when a member of jail staff came with smiling

face and whispered that my release order had arrived at jail and I was about to leave. I confirmed that it was an official message. Therefore, I wrapped up my small things, like two to three suits only, in a shopping bag and got ready for the final call to leave.

Meanwhile, the good news was also communicated to my kids. A car sent by Rohi with her personal driver waited outside the jail to take us to her home, where we were to live.

It was winter; my children and I got into the car and said goodbye to everyone and asked all to forgive us if we had hurt anybody. The jail superintendent lady appreciated our conduct remained unoffending and that we had all been compliant inmates who had never ever caused any problems nor ever became part of any problem of politics inside the jail.

These words were energising for me as I had done nothing in my life which could have been seen and felt by anyone other than myself but this was the first time for me hearing the words from someone else that kept watch on me and kept observing my conduct. Innocence was my identity and criminality of any kind never ever appealed to me.

I was leaving bondage. I was on my way to freedom. I was set free. I was feeling alleviated. I felt like I was walking on air. Beyond any iota of doubt words fail me to share how much my freedom warmed the cockles of my heart.

I also felt warm and fuzzy while walking the green mile and expecting to meet someone I had long cherished in my raw feelings. Perhaps, I was whistling past the graveyard as uncertainty of all kinds awaited for me.

Deeply entrenched in guesswork, I ultimately reached Rohi's home in Karachi; it was an old, grand, Victorian-style house covering two to three acres of land with a big lawn, bird corner, swimming pool, waterfalls and old trees with spread wings.

For a while my mind went into a fantastic world of arts where everything appeared picture-perfect.

On my arrival at her home, Rohi warmly welcomed me. She had bought lots of things for me including new clothes, jewellery, shoes, cosmetics and other things of daily use. She also took me to a parlour and changed my get-up altogether.

She further emphasized that I was to live like an urban women, keep on learning and join a gym for physical fitness as Rohi herself was a very stylish and fit woman.

I was amazed at her hospitality. More important than all these items were the words that Rohi uttered for welcoming me. She said: 'Dear Hoor, this house belongs to your sister in soul, though not in blood, Rohi, who is the sole owner of these premises. Never feel alien here. Take it as your own home of your own heart mates and relax till your life course is streamlined. I promise you to get your life on track in a similar way as I have got you released. Credit also goes to my friend Jibraan for having put his own spin on your case, as he is a famous human rights activist also. You must be feeling elevated and should be on cloud nine for this!'

Rohi further acquainted me. 'I have a complete plan for your education, your lifestyle, your employment and your social activities. In the next few days we will be having meetings with people from different walks of life because I want to tell the world, how strange it is that in this age of human rights, innocence of the weakest in society is being brutally punished; power cows down justice; inhumanity imprisons peace; male dominance makes trust feel shy in marital bonding; the damn system makes helplessness dance to its tunes; the resourceless person hardly finds hope anywhere in the present system of state and society as a whole. Therefore, we are here to explore hope within ourselves instead of waiting for any help from outside to reach us.'

So, as a consequence of our bonding in spirituality, intellectuality and ideology, I and Rohi joined hands to work for the honour and dignity of womenfolk in all walks of life from household to leadership. I had a story to tell the world, while Rohi had resources for presenting my case full well on all national as well as international forums.

# Chapter Twenty-Four

After two days rest and discussions at Rohi's home, she called Jibraan to pay a visit to her home, informing him about my stay and the circumstances at her end. Jibraan was away for some days on his personal assignments and he committed to come at the weekend.

That Sunday came finally. Jibraan was to come in the early morning to have breakfast with us. We were in the kitchen busy making something special for him. I was good at cooking.

Rohi told me Jibraan's favourite dish was fresh fruit juice, fruit chaat, Chinese noodles and tea mixed with milk. I was perfect at making tea mixed with milk and also fresh juices but also learnt to prepare noodles.

I was waiting for the appearance of a man I had long cherished to see and to meet. Words fail me to describe how the current of his presence ran through my nerves like lighting on the sky. My heart was going out of my body; my brain had stuck, stopping speculation but had gone static with little audible whispers which kept on echoing my mind with self-talk that, 'Hoor you are about to meet your love'.

I started biting my tongue the very moment the bell rang and a house servant informed that, 'Mr Jibraan has come; should I bring him to the drawing room?'

Rohi herself went out to receive him and to bring him

inside the lounge. I was standing in her open kitchen facing the TV lounge.

Jibraan smiled at me on first sight and said, 'Hi.' This came to me as a cool breeze to neutralize my excitement. For a while, I started thinking that the whole the world was smiling and happiness was blooming all around with showering flowers everywhere in the sky.

I was in a topsy-turvy state. Though I raised my eyebrows, yet I felt a little shy to show up my inner self very quickly. I also tried to respond with same eagerness, feeling very warm and fuzzy. I went into the state of mind that my life had an end that had happened by then and I had in mind nothing outside and nothing beyond that magic man called Jibraan Khan.

He was a tall, 5ft 11in, fair-skinned, jet-black-haired, lightly bearded, well-built man in his late thirties, and wearing western dress of two pieces.

For me everything very special was happening that Sunday and I had made up my mind to bare my soul to Jibraan and tell him all that I had long kept under wraps. However, it was very hard for me to cork up everything in that very first meeting but I was beside myself in utter excitement to tell him all the torments and woes I had undergone over the years.

My own entity started duplicating, creating and recreating the chain of its own images to behave in an impressive manner with the man who I was not sure to prevail on. My mind engine was working on its all cylinders to find the way of speaking my heart to my idol and explore the words to let him know as to how I found him and began to love him at the time when he was quite unaware of such love in making. Nor yet I had any hope of seeing and meeting him any time in my life.

But that Sunday, this all was happening as a natural course.

When I was with Rohi and Jibraan, Jibraan addressed me, saying in his first ever face-to-face exchange of words: 'I don't know much about you personally. However, I need to know a lot about you for my own consumption as an artist and as a human rights activist. I am sure your case could win many women in the world their cases, which are hanging in balance due to lack of logic, interest, and evidence. I can very clearly see everything written all over your face which mirrors your heart.'

Taking long breaths, having my eyes down, I was moving my head up and down very slowly. However, in a few seconds, I was just galvanized and my body movements were getting electrified with the passion of love. At the same time all the storm I had been weathering all along began to rewind in my mind, making my heart go doleful and achy.

In order to normalise my mood, Jibraan said: 'Rohi, where is the food, I feel famished and hunger is voicing protests.' I stood up but Rohi stopped me saying that the cook would set the table. Cook did and we all three started the food at the dining table. I was not well accustomed to dining manners but following what Rohi was doing, I started slowly. They were talking and eating like anything as if this was their last breakfast but I due to my ignorance of eating manners was a bit confused to keep pace with them, though I did try. In fifteen minutes or so we finished and Jibraan asked me: 'Hoor, should I expect to know about your story today or come some other day?' I replied: 'No one is sure to see tomorrow. What I can do today, I don't leave for tomorrow and what I am to do tomorrow, I like to do today because I can't put time under my spell. 'At this he smiled and said: 'You are really smarter than I had thought you could be!'

Jibraan further asked me, 'Should we move to the lawn and

sit next to the waterfall where I would feel cool and would like you to narrate me your tale, making sky, earth, water and all of nature witness to the truth of your life.' I consented finding the idea very appealing.

With tea, pen and paper, Jibraan and I were in front of the waterfall on the lawn sitting on fabric chairs under umbrella-shade to save ourselves from the sun's heat.

He told me he knew everything about my story as he was the author of the commission report and a very key member who had already highlighted my story in the commission report.

He referred to the commission in which my story emerged as its animating and moving spirit: 'Many analysts and critics of the commission have called the commission report a very powerful message to all corners only because of the dominant story of Hoor, who really mirrors the lacunas in our systems of all kinds and is very revealing as to how we treat our women and what we really are as human beings.'

He showed his personal keen interest in knowing me: 'I personally want to know you more than I want to know the details of your story. I remember your interview with the commission. You left us all asking ourselves as to how conscientious we were and how civilized were the society we were members of! Your case was very telling, very revealing, very identifying, very striking and very challenging for the social norms, cultural values, and statutory laws.'

He said that my case became the case study of the commission exposing all segments of society ranging from family, community, private and state criminal justice mechanisms in our country, freedom, rights, culture, traditions, and dogmas to the extent of challenging their worth and justifications.

Over to Jibraan, 'We documented and presented many cases and your case was the recurrent theme of our findings as your case was crystal-clear without any iota of doubt that you were innocent and a great injustice was done to you by family, society, and also state. Your case made us feel and highlight the innate discriminations, biases, and inherent weaknesses in our all man-made systems of society and state.'

Further assuring all kind of help Jibraan wanted to know my expectations from him and Rohi. He owned: 'I am here to know about you and what you expect us, me and Rohi, to do for you. What are your plans for the future? Rest assured we are with you. Take care of yourself as you and your kids are by now our common responsibility. We will do our level best for you.'

I thanked Jibraan for extending his help. I told him: 'I have been waiting to tell you what I have not had the opportunity to tell you before.' He responded: 'Sure, please.' I was shivering slightly but trying to show that I was damn clear, confident and categorical in my expression about what was I feeling.

I voiced: 'My heart is for you. You rule my heartland. Through your writings and ideas, you have very successfully punctuated my entity. You are now the undisputed and only prince whose signature or control is unrivalled in my ocean of emotions and world of dreams. I love you and accept you with all your faults, limits, and weaknesses as my first and last love in this short sojourn of life on earth.'

Further ventilating my heart, I continued.

'This time, I will not narrate the story nor yet you write the tale of our love but the orator-writer lovers' tale will be preserved by others in times to come. I don't know whether it would be possible for you to accept me in this love format but I am down for it. This is, perhaps, the grooviest moment in my life which I am feeling and enjoying as if I have been able to live the centuries of my love with my beloved in this short span!'

Jibraan had a static smile on what I was expressing. He exploded his heart with the burning pellets of love emotions which were long smouldering in him: 'I have waited for my love for a long time and I never thought it could come to me the way it has! I can feel the genuineness of your revelation of love, faith in your feelings, enormity of your emotions, and truth of your love.'

Jibraan welcomed my love with these words.

'I accept you with all your realities and let me tell you it is not only you who cherished me as your dream man but the day I saw you and came to know your story, you have not left my mind even for a while to have a break from thinking about you. You did not go out of my consciousness. I kept thinking and thinking about you as to how people victimized you. However, the beauty of your character and personality was evident from the fact that despite having undergone a long period of pangs you kept smiling.'

Jibraan came clean about his long desire of finding his soul-mate.

'Perhaps, I waited for you till this date and perhaps I liked no one because you were somewhere waiting and cherishing me. Today is the day we strike no deal, ask no questions, make no demands, keep no conditions, go for no formalities but to admit that we have found our love and that we are for each other for all the times to come and for all the time we are left to live. We are welded together. We shall wed too.'

I hugged him fast and he wrapped me in his arms. I was curled around him like ivy. My eyes began to shower and I

147

started crying inside. He was consoling me and saying, 'Be patient this is human life; we are not robots.'

Jibraan mitigated me in a very altitudinous manner, 'You should be proud for what you have done on your own at your own end, and you, therefore, need not regret what has been done to you. We leave this to society and state to regret on all that they have been doing with so many females since time immemorial. Your case will go a long way in changing the paradigm of state authority and social values.'

Jibraan stated in a very prideful mood.

'I am going to make your story go viral and global so that everyone could see on their smart phones worldwide as to what we are doing with our females in this part of the world and how stalwart are our females, despite their being caught up in the throes of a very hostile system.'

However, Jibraan asked me for some time to convince his parents about our case. Despite being very liberal, Jibraan was a perfect family man who never wanted to hurt his mom and dad. But for himself he assured me full well that he was for me in all senses. I was happy with that and could live my remaining life on these words of Jibraan whom I loved beyond anyone's wildest dreams. He met with my children. He loved them and left. I stood at the door to wave my hand of hope that my future or my happiness was there for me.

# Chapter Twenty-Five

After six weeks Rohi and I were all alone and dining outside at some restaurant on the seashore. There were dim lights and the restaurant seemed very cosy and romantic.

Rohi asked me, 'How was your meeting with Jibraan?'

I told her, 'It went very well and I found him a man of meaning, even much better than the idea I had about him.'

'That is great. Jibraan had the same views about you,' Rohi explained, 'and a very important thing that I noted was that when I asked him about your humble education, Jibraan came with very clear thought and assured, 'Education is not my criteria or condition and I can get Hoor educated but I can't ever form a person's character the way I have seen in this woman."

'Jabe further said,' Rohi told me; 'I was in search of her and found her at my doorstep. This is really a miracle for me. She is one who is a true 'speciwoman' of true feminine power and vision.'

Rohi continued quoting Jibraan, 'Despite all odds,' said Jabe, 'Hoor is damn confident and has faith in herself to make things better for her while apparently having no resources available at hand, nor does she expect us to do things very urgently but the beauty of hers is the attitude and body language indicating her full trust in all her relations, including me and you. Whatever, but her confidence is yet to be decomposed for the belief that something good will happen to her from somewhere and she will be able to pull in her torments and troubles.'

Rohi kept running on further, 'Your attitude of confidence and good composition of your moods is killing and has killed Jabe. Frankly, he is no more Jibraan; he is the lover of Hoor. So you are very lucky to have been the love of such a noble soul who has taken a long time to like someone that is what I personally know about him.'

Rohi asked me: 'What do you have in mind for the rest of your life? Will you be going back to your village or what are you planning for your kids?' After a silence and a thought about what I should say to her, because I had not yet thought anything about that, I said: 'My daughter wants to be a singer and she has a pretty good and sweet voice and my son wishes to be a cop. Let me see how I will be able to manage all this!'

'That is a good idea,' Rohi said, 'I heard your daughter singing while sitting on the lawn yesterday. Her voice is really sweet and awesome. Your son is also smart, well built and tall. I know some senior police officers and their families so I will do my best to get him appointed in the police. The idea of putting your son in the police is perfect as you and your family would feel a little more protected and secure.'

Rohi asked me to make a choice of food from the menu of the restaurant. I told her that I was really restless to eat fish and mutton *Karhai* with *Rogni naan* (Bread) followed by ice-cream *falluda*.

She laughed and said, 'Today my menu is the same and though I very rarely take mutton, this time I want to go with your choice.' We both enjoyed the food and liked the spot.

On our way back in the car, which Rohi was driving, she opened a discussion about the type of relation I wanted to have with Jibraan. On this, I replied, 'I love him and I don't know how far we could go in a relationship!' Rohi observed: 'You seem to be helpless at the hands of your heart. You have seen loneliness over eight years in jail and the devil must be dancing in your mind for having some love and romance.'

'No, my sweetie, I am not that much close to the devil,' I assured her. 'It is because of my being at loggerheads with the devil that I keep up suffering upon suffering which have very religiously and passionately followed my tracks in life; it is aptly presumed that bad guys hardly suffer in this world of humans but it has always been good guys who have gone through all types of ordeals and hardest tests of cruel time.'

I further exposed my notions, 'I have paid a big price for my goodness, while I have seen many people whom badness has paid tremendously. Therefore, my experience of dealing with human feelings has taught me that goodness always needs to be paid for while badness pays most of the time. My heart goes for love, not for love making!'

Rohi commented in utter surprise with a loud tone 'I see! You know how to play with words, not only how to engage emotions.'

'Is that a compliment or a criticism?' I enquired of her, while feeling a little uncomfortable with her ultra-frankness.

Rohi clarifying her views uttered very politely, 'Please don't get me wrong. I mean to say that you very beautifully explain your ideas and express your feelings.'

I commented, 'Thank you very much for all this and I suppose you would not mind nor should you have any concern for me and Jibraan as I don't want to hurt a person (you) who stood for me in my bad time.'

While on our way home, Rohi called Jibraan and asked him about his whereabouts. He was near so she invited him home. He arrived at Rohi's home after we got in there. We met in the car porch and entered the house together. Rohi seemed a bit uneasy and a little infuriated about my inappropriate question.

Rohi asked Jibraan, 'Jabe can you explain our relationship to Hoor, who has some doubts which I want to clear up as she trusts you.' Jabe said: 'We are friends, not lovebirds.' Jabe stated categorically, 'I think this should suffice.' He further asked me: 'Is there any problem?'

I said, 'There is no problem at all and Rohi has got annoyed about my inappropriate question which I did not ask with any wrong intent. I am a woman with a long list of torments and sufferings at the hands of the system so I have my own inner insecurities, the lead being jealousy with your ultra-frankness with Rohi, who I take as my sister and to whom I am indebted for a lot more things including my freedom and dignity.'

I continued, 'But my fears of losing you made me stone-blinded. Now I stand clear because of your and Rohi's understanding of my woes and fears. I apologize for my mistake and I trust you both as the only people in my small world that I love and who mean a lot to me.'

Jibraan went straight to hug Rohi and requested her to accept my apology and she did by hugging me with tears. Her being hurt broke me like anything because I was wrong and I should not have asked such a question in that wrongly worded way.

Jibraan said: 'Okay, relax everybody, mis-wording and misstatement should not be mixed and you both are very noble women and I don't want you to continue with this 'shockwave' anymore. I need a cup of tea and who will make it for me?' Both I and Rohi smiled and rushed to the kitchen to make three cups of tea. I told Rohi to attend to Jibraan while I made the tea the way Jibraan liked.

While I was making tea I heard Jibraan and Rohi talking about me through a window which connected the kitchen and the lounge.

Jibraan while consoling Rohi requested her, 'Rohi I am really sorry for what Hoor questioned you about as you are my best buddy and have always stood by me even in my bad times. Above all you are a noble lady. I appreciate the way you have responded and handled Hoor's concerns. Had there been any other lady in your place she should have given perfect peace of mind to Hoor but I salute you for your magnanimity, your patience, your humanity and most importantly your calibre of womanhood. Again please accept her apology.'

Rohi while weeping deep inside and with disturbed breaths and tears falling in fast sequence voiced: 'Jabe, I am a human being and also a woman. Though deeply moved by Hoor's inappropriate questioning and doubting, I am quite clear that her intention was never wrong and it is but natural in love to feel jealous seeing her lover or loved one taking interest in something other than her. I have gone through all this and I can understand it. However, I wish Hoor had never asked this to me. I would not never ever make this unfortunate moment an issue nor would I keep this in my heart because I am the type of person who could never ever afford to live with neither burdens of the heart nor tensions of the mind. I have a lighter heart and tender mind. So, I have no issue of this sort with your Hoor anymore!'

Jibraan appreciating Rohi's big heart in accepting my

apology explained my case to Rohi in these words: 'I appreciate full well the way you take Hoor. But let me tell you what Hoor really is! Hoor is not merely beautiful in terms of the etymological meaning of her name. She is a beautiful mixture of woman, beauty and innocence.'

On this Rohi explained my physical beauty to Jibraan: 'Her everything is just perfect despite having been deprived of a proper education and life conditions and having been hard hit by two forced marriages, childbearing and other consequences of losing husbands, howsoever they were, and families, she still has a gorgeous physical appearance with her big hazel eyes with naturally made-up thin and fine eyebrows, with her slim and straight nose, with her mango-slice lips, with honey-brown hair, with a long neck like a white water bird, with a broad and tall body having no extra flesh at any part and a height of 5ft 8in and weight of 62kg and with red-pink skin colour like red Indians. This is what she looks like outside.'

Rohi's appreciated me in this way: 'No doubt, Hoor's appearance is stunning but still ravishing is her inner person – her character. She has a very lively conscience, clean heart, creative mind and a very positive thinking. She has her own rules of life which she has developed over the years with her troubles in life her main source of learning and the system her leading teacher. She is as pure as angels but she takes her womanhood as her power despite the fact she has gone through continuous victimization on that very ground of being a woman, who is taken as a weak entity, undoubtedly, in our systems of all kinds. But her feature of personality that outstands and dominates is her virgin love for you, Jabe. Like a true woman, Hoor entertains pure feelings. She loves and she continues to love till death. I have seen in her eyes the flicker of rare inspiration to walk barefoot on burning coals for you.'

Jibraan held my struggle with high esteem: 'Her war with the mighty system and its sub-systems has damaged to some extent, indeed, but has not been able to break her iron-built entity. She is challenger and sufferer who never surrenders her fight with the system but keeps her eagle eyes straight to her self-chosen destiny of fighting for liberating the womenfolk of our part of the world from the chains of man-made systems of society, culture, and state. She represents the voice against women victimization.'

Rohi declares me a revolutionary female character.

'She is firmer and her very existence and survival is something like a silent feminist revolution greatly fuelled by her story as a gospel of undeniable truth. She has fallen victim to the system and so is a role model for all those women who are not happy with their conditions. However, she is remarkably different from the women who, being unhappy with their circumstances, wait for miracles to happen but rather she believes that her woes are born out of the system and do not come from her destiny. So instead of waiting for any celestial power to work miracles, the womenfolk should engage the system with the intention of correcting it the way some parts of human civilizations on earth have very successfully done. She believes improving the lot of women is a doable thing. I really wonder having seen such willpower and such forbearance in a woman like Hoor. This is, indeed, a rare thing to reckon with in today's world of shortcuts and ready-made solutions and is a lesson for females like us who wish to roll in luxuries.'

Jibraan added to Rohi's description of 'me', Hoor, with these words: 'I am in complete accord with your very apt remarks about the beauties of Hoor; however, there are still many good things in the person of Hoor, a towering name, a rising fame, a glowing lady, an emerging trend, a challenging voice, a silent revolution, a force behind building a new system and also an opportunity to make history of new culture and a new system in our country. There are and have been many victims of the system like Hoor but unlike Hoor they did not raise their voice nor try to challenge their circumstance. Consequently, their tales went unheard and their courage unsung.'

Rohi agreed with Jibraan saying:

'Just look at Hoor's circumstance, her marriage was decided by her parents long before she was born, she married, bore children, became a widow and was remarried at gunpoint. Everything in her life happened without her will but rather forcibly but what is great is that she never accepted at heart all that happened to her. She was jailed for eight long years for the crimes of others. She was never guilty nor was she found guilty at the end of the day. Nobody in the system answers anyone of us as to who will return Hoor her eight years that she lost just for nothing.'

Rohi further credited ,'However, eight years of an innocent woman in jail made headlines and stories in the media which has become a legend: heard, told and sung in every home of Pakistan to show the solidarity with all women victims of violence and victimization of all types. What has happened to her was all without her consent and without her fault.'

Jibraan nodded and responded to what Rohi was saying in this way: 'Everything in her life remained non-consensual and forcible. She neither co-existed with violence and torture but never ever let herself down nor compromised with hostile circumstances of life which outstood her all along. Hoor is our legend, a role model and an example to follow while she holds no degree from Harvard University nor yet belongs to the silver screen yet she is the best example of the power of the woman, representing her own voice which can create ripples and can rock the very foundations of the system we are living in.'

I knocked and they went silent but Jibraan said: 'Rohi was talking about the life your role has infused in feminist voices in Pakistan.' We took the tea and Jibraan left after having tea and planning for the job of my kids and me.

# Chapter Twenty-Six

Rohi was very good at heart; that was quite vivid from speaking her heart with Jibraan in my absence. I regretted hurting Rohi, a very clean-hearted lady.

Therefore, when we dispersed and I became alone, I made a phone call to Jibraan from my cell phone. I revealed all my inner insecurities to him very honestly and frankly with an admission that no one could ever do for me what Rohi had done and that I had no reservations if Rohi entertained some feelings about Jibraan but my concern that was cooking up inside me was because of Rohi's very informal relation with Jibraan.

This had become the cause of concern for me and I wanted to know the actual facts! Jibraan was very candid to tell me from very beginning, Rohi had remained his best friend since their university life and that she was the best woman in all terms especially humanity.

Jibraan further confirmed that Rohi was a filthy-rich woman with a strong family background and Jibraan was from a humble family background. So Jibraan never entertained a desire to think of loving her but he always respected her.

When Jibraan's life attained some significance due to his rise to an intellectual and a writer of high calibre with a celebrated fame and with a smiling fortune, Rohi had gone much ahead in marrying, and remarrying. However, under all tribulations and torments of Rohi's life, he stood with her as an inspiration for her.

Rohi had many commonalities with me in terms of marital experience. We both married two times and had children. Our age was the same with many similar face and body features and thoughts. She was *Nazik*, with a soft and sensitive body and a wise heart but I had the same soft heart with a tough body. Jibraan was also our common factor with our motivation to do something for womenfolk in Pakistan. We both idealized him as our perfect man and Jibraan also rated us the best women.

However, it became crystal clear to me that Jibraan loved me and he liked Rohi as his best friend ever. I also understood that no one takes care of me as well as Rohi did of Jibraan. Therefore, for Jibraan and for me, Rohi was part of our personal life, indeed. This was the fact I understood from what I discussed with Jibraan. Jibraan and Rohi both loved me. Rohi never minded my being in love with Jibraan.

Rohi was a very fair lady. She loved me and respected me like anything. Though both of us were females, we loved each other almost equally well. In addition, Rohi used to bear all my expenses until I got to earn myself. We both were more important for each other in all terms. We lived together for a few years. She educated, cultured, and civilized me, making me true human stuff.

Apart from my grooming, Rohi managed to get my son appointed in the police department and got my daughter introduced to 'Voice-Studio', a nursery for singers in Karachi where my daughter Zuhra participated in competitions and won the top position in Karachi. In that competition my daughter had sung my own written songs. There had been two different stages to win and to sing different and new songs. I wrote both songs for her and she won. I am giving hereunder the lyrics of my songs with translation in English.

### Songs written by Hoor and sung by
### her daughter Zuhra:

Song 1: Lyrics
**TITLE: THE DAUGHTER OF THE LAND OF PURE**
**I am the daughter of the land of pure;**
**I am made up of the soil, very pure.**
1. My heart is clean & my entity is innocent;
My system conspires to keep me ignorant.
I feel it to the core.
2. My destiny smiles always;
The tune of my heart, it plays.
To me, the emotions lure.
3. My woes, my rows, & my foes are system's gifts;
With my own being & destiny, I have no rifts.
But ahead I foresee deep mire.
4. Peace, Justice, & progress, I dream, they prevail;
This opportunity, I wish, my soldiers, cops, and patriots must avail.
Before things, at home, get dire!
Oh my soul mate, oh my heartbeat rescue my innocence;
Oh my lifeline, oh my mind match eliminate my impuissance. For the reason in point, I need a saviour.
I am the daughter of the land of pure; I am made up of the soil, very pure.
WRITTEN BY HOOR; SUNG BY ZUHRA

Song 2: Lyrics
**TITLE: YOU ARE IN ME**

160

**In me, in my madness, you make your appearance**;
In my consciousness, in my inner peace, and
In my every breath, you show your presence;
In my pain, in my prayers and in every corner of my heart,
You stand in elegance.
In my memories, in my visions, and
In my yearning, you appear in reverence.
WIRTTEN BY Hoor; SUNG BY ZUHRA

# Chapter Twenty-Seven

It was Monday morning. Rohi had just got up. She checked me on the intercom and I was also up. She called me to have breakfast together. I got there in ten minutes. She was in a nightdress and making eggs for breakfast. I asked her to let me make the food but she said: 'Today, I make it and if you are so keen to assist me then please make tea.'

Very quickly, I began to make tea and we placed edibles on the kitchen table and both sat face to face after everything was ready. Rohi asked me about whether I had talked to Jabe. I said yes I did yesterday. This raised my anxiety and I asked her whether everything was fine.

She said she was just asking as 'Jibraan was busy trying to seek a contract with some international magazines for his writings. He had submitted his particulars to some very well reputed forums. He got offers from more than one corner so he was a bit confused which one to go for.'

Meanwhile, I saw Rohi's mobile ringing with 'Jabe calling' on her screen. She smiled and said loudly, 'Call the devil and the devil is there; we were talking about Jibraan and he called. In our folk logic, when we remember someone he either appears physically or makes a phone call to one who remembers him or her; that person, who either calls or appears is presumed to live long.'

She picked up the phone and started talking, 'Hello Jabe

how is everything? Let me tell you that you will live long as I and Hoor were discussing you at breakfast as to where you have gone, perhaps you're quite busy in the publication of your new works.'

Rohi set her call on speaker mode and I heard Jibraan saying in quite a happy mood, 'You and Hoor have no topic other than poor Jibraan so keep on condemning him for nothing, hahaha.' Rohi reacted a bit comically while I smiling face. His observation about us touched our conscience and consciousness. He was right in what he said. On this Rohi told him, 'All our roads lead to Jibran'.

She continued discussing with him his options and offers; while hearing him my heart was blooming in the port of happiness as if I was in seventh heaven. I was in a mental state of emotional transition. I began to recall my difficult days. I began to think of a man who had conquered my heart. I ultimately met and fell in love with him who is now just a call away from me.

Besides this, all my hopes had flourished into a reality of breaking the shackles of bondage and slavery-like scenarios; I had been made to suffer. I never considered Jibraan as my victory but I took him as my inner peace that was worth my struggle.

Finally, Jibraan and Rohi came to the conclusion that Jibraan should opt for a UK-based international magazine, *Gender-Times,* which focuses on issues of women's rights.

Jibraan was appointed as country correspondent and analyst for Pakistan to take all the wrongs done to the womenfolk in Pakistan. And Jibraan sought my permission to start his international career with my story which he had titled *Whiter than White.*

I was more than happy that my man had got that much insight about me and a great appreciation for what and how I have been dealing with in my own way. I, just in a happy mood, asked him, 'What will be the story brief or abstract which you are going to write on me?' He stated that the promo of his story titled *Whiter than White* would go like this:

'*Whiter Than White* is a story portraying the true power of a woman through its lead character Hoor who is completely honest, perfectly innocent, extremely clean, absolutely brave, highly strong, impeccably loyal and immaculately legendary in all that she has been doing since her birth despite being put to all kinds of hostile conditions of life by the system, culture, state and the society in our part of the world.'

I asked him, 'Is it really real?' Jibraan said in a strange mood, 'It is more than real.' I told him, 'Nobody knows me that much; so it sounds fictitious!' Jibraan said with confidence and very categorically, 'All fiction is born out of real life and every creative human being whether a designer, an architect, a singer, a writer or whoever, always thinks within the possibilities of what he or she has heard, seen, and experienced. Fiction is about life and life is what we live. How we live it teaches us how we should live it. Thus, every fiction work is one way or the other linked to real life and so is true with my story: *Whiter than White.*'

This answer was satisfactory but my curiosity did not stop there and inched ahead with another question: 'Why did you title my story *Whiter than White* and what does this expression mean?'

He replied very eagerly: '*Whiter than White* is an English idiom or idiomatic expression which is used as an adjective and which means innocent, clean, flawless, perfect and pure. I believe this expression fits your character, so I go for it.'

Being highly astounded, I did put into words: 'you are not only a good human being, a good friend, a good thinker, an excellent writer but also an outstanding lover who has ideas and emotions to kill anybody, especially women.'

On this he laughed uncontrollably and brought out: 'I am not that much of a romantic killer, as you feel about me; had I been, many might have been killed to date but my score is very poor in that! Only one or two, including you because I always needed one for whom I waited. Finally we are together.'

Our phone call of about forty minutes ended, Rohi and I went to our rooms to freshen up.

# Chapter Twenty-Eight

After Two Months

Jibraan joined *Gender-Times*. His first story titled *Whiter than White* was published. He wrote the story of my life. He portrayed me, Hoor, a powerful character who despite the worst conditions and having thin hope of salvation fought her circumstances with confidence, courage, boldness, and faith in herself. She was full of wit and vivacity.

Many newspapers and TV channels were teeming with praise of Jibraan's *Whiter than White* in which he had made a 'strong case against the system' as one of the analysts commented on his story.

There were others who called it, 'the most powerful feminist voice' raised in a culture of male dominance, rooted well and deep into the traditions, the culture, the society, and also the folklore.

Still others praised the plot of his story as 'a well-knit scheme of thought, well-linked events, noble purpose, and sterling choice of words, univocal expression, thrilling beginning, illuminating end and also the supernal morale.'

Likewise, Jibraan's first introductory sentence became the most quoted sentence of wisdom and expression, which read: 'In life when the going gets tough, believe you me, the tough gets going like anything.' His other very witty comment in the story included: 'We have to live in a damn system where power cows down justice; inhumanity imprisons peace; resourcefulness plays hell with helplessness; and brutality molests innocence.'

One of the leading papers of our country, the *Telegram*, wrote in its review of the story of Jibraan: 'Jibraan's pen is magical and his mind is a magnet which has attracted gender truths from the remotest, the most ignored areas and people to the limelight of the world. He is a proven gem that continues to produce the reflections of the multiple colours of causes which make the life of women in this part of the globe a bed of thorns.'

The *Telegram* continued: 'His efforts to explore the tales of innocence immortalized and incriminated are worth a new discovery of a new discourse on the rights of women. He discovers themes vicariously instead of inventing them rigorously. Even in his discovery of Hoor with lots of thematic decor, he has gone far ahead in adding his spices of genius to this story, *Whiter than White*.'

On a famous English talk show: *Rights for Right or Right for Rights* on Vision TV networks, the renowned anchor person Jan Shah speaking about *Whiter Than White* maintained: 'To me, *Whiter Than White* is not the story of a fiction, nor yet merely a fact file of a woman victim of multiple violations and crimes committed by all and sundry against her but rather a charge-sheet against dark spots of our culture, dogmas of our folklore, traditions of family and community systems, vulnerabilities of the rotten social system, the weaknesses of policing and investigations, discriminations and fault-lines of our criminal justice system to offer a required protection to females against highhandedness of male members, against falling victim to traditions of culture, against greed of law officers, and against coercive authority of the state.'

Jan Shah kept going: 'The situation of gender anarchy leaves us hopeless and women helpless to do anything for bringing change while living in this system. But Jibraan finds the solution in woman's own power – which to him is the power of all powers of humanity. His lead character, Hoor, represents the same powers.'

One of the guest speakers in Jan Shah's program, Sardar Ahmad, considered *Whiter Than White*, 'A universal call for the "association of consciences" to raise the issue of women's woes caused by the systems in place and which are never natural, never celestial, never divine, never by default but rather by pure nefarious design, man-made, earthly, and a worst product of the system.'

Secondly, another guest speaker, Gulraiz Khan, proposed: '*Whiter Than White* is a mirror of the prevalence of deep-laid gender discrimination, biases, and injustices in our state's justice delivery system and in our society's cultural traditions, it is, therefore, a high time for the media, government, non-government organizations, and also international community/ organizations to pool sum total of their wisdom to reason out a "way-out" for the women victims of diversified crimes, which have taken deep roots in our society and which grow and glow unhindered because of the weaknesses, vulnerabilities and misunderstanding of our culture, law, traditions, folklore and also religious cults.'

Jan Shah in a very bemoaning tone summarized *Whiter than White* as follows:

'*Whiter than White*, a story of Hoor, a female character, by Jibraan Khan, clearly reveals the massive victimization of the woman in Pakistan. It paints a horrible picture wherein it is shown with alarming clarity as to how the tradition of honour killing plays hell with the innocent lives of both the dead as well as survivors and as to how private and parallel justice systems take away the fundamental rights of the people in general and that of the woman in particular.'

Shah further threw light on *Whiter than White* with these words:

'It also throws enough light on the indifference of our governmental system that leaves the weaker vessel at the mercy of the cruel decisions of the *sardars* and *waderas* (local notables). This, indeed, reflects the grave tragedy of emotion wherein the woman, who is endowed with all human faculties, is left without any option to decide about herself but to live up to the whims and caprices of her males. To me, she seems to be the victim of inscribed slavery, imposed hardships, veiled lifestyle, and engineered silence in our country. Uninterrupted victimization of women has become one of the leading problems of our times. This phenomenon sends clear signals to every conscientious person to believe that the victimization of the woman in Pakistan is, indeed, a sad tale of culture and system.'

Furthering his programme Mr Shah finally made a general comment on the situation of the womenfolk in Pakistan with these words: 'It goes without saying that the violence and discriminations against the woman are commonplace in our society. The woman faces massive resistance for everything. If it is the matter of property, honour, or personal animosity of different tribes or people, the woman serves as the best scapegoat for them to settle their scores.'

My case was declared by Jan Shah to be a glaring example

of all the problems of womenfolk in Pakistan. He maintained:

'Countless women suffer from domestic violence, parental pressures, spousal abuse, forced marriages, unjustified divorces, sexual assaults, burning acid attacks, mutilation, rape and battery. The case of Hoor is symbol of the victimization of all kinds in our society. Therefore, Jibraan's discovery and making it public in a splendid way deserves all kinds of accolades.'

This is only the tip of the iceberg of accolades, laurels and homage paid to Jibraan's work of *Whiter than White*. I, being the lead character of his story, was also feeling jubilant on all that at least my life, which has been full of difficulties and replete with tensions all over, has become an international story with appreciation of how I deal with my realities and how I kept my balances, senses and high spirits throughout the rough and tumbles of my life. Hardly anyone can imagine, but only I myself, the feeling of beatitude and blissfulness for being acknowledged and acclaimed for the pains I bore, difficulties I faced, troubles I encountered, discriminations I suffered and the chill wind of the woes I felt.

# Chapter Twenty-Nine

Jibraan became famous with his new discourse on woman's capacity to revive, determination to survive, wisdom to thrive and motivation to relive a life converted by the damn circumstances of it. Jibraan wanted to tell something about women in an idiomatic and unprecedented way. And beyond doubt he succeeded in realising his dream.

I wanted to be heard by a tender heart and receptive ear. Ultimately, all our spiritual, emotional, intellectual, intuitive, instinctive, sensual and social roads led us to one point of eternal union. The circumstances threw us at a point of being partners. I saw in him my own voice and my own shadow and he found his own eloquent ideal in me that he was very articulately looking for!

I reached the state of mind that my life closed on meeting Jibraan, while Jibraan embarked upon presuming that his life had just begun to rack up true meaning and to score victory in exploring as well as publishing my story. How strange is life! How cruel is time! How ruthless is the system! How beautiful is destiny. Despite the conspiracies of birth, genesis, time, and system, destiny designed our eternal union plan, bringing colours to my life.

Not my destiny, but the system I was born and lived in tried to destroy my womanhood. Statutory laws and cultural norms were hand in glove with each other to betray me against the highhandedness of male imperium. Statutory laws beguiled me when I was victimized by the cultural traditions. Nothing gave me more tingles than my own dearest and nearest ones, including my parents, siblings, and blood relatives.

However, throughout my life, innocence is what has really defined my identity; compliance, not deviance, has been the hallmark of my personality; conformity, not criminality, has always appealed me but as ill luck would have it, I have hardly been able to blaze the trail of my freedom. It always sounded logical and sensible that 'people are created to be loved and things to be used but most people I see use other fellows instead of loving them.'

To my very good luck, Jibraan was the other way round. He was not run of the mill but the cream of humanity who loved a woman like me just on one single ground that, to him, I appeared to be a true woman, not even a perfect woman. Most of the chaps run after perfection while there are only few and far between, like Jibraan, who hanker after truth. So, both I and Jibraan were on the same page regarding our union of true man and true woman striving for truth, an activity which always taxes and costs for which we were prepared, perhaps, since we matured to our senses and meanings.

Whatever our visions tell us and how educative our insights may seem, we have to systematize and can't live in space or in a vacuum but among the people in their systems and culture where marriage and family have stood the test of time. Having that in mind Jibraan proposed to marry me. I consented without any pre-thought.

He was the only son of his parents, having no sister and no brother. His mother, named ZarGul, was a retired principal of a college and was in her mid-sixties. His father, Mr Zamran Khan, was also a retired civil officer from the army and in his late sixties. They lived a retired life in their house at Bath Island, Karachi. Their entire world was Jibraan. All their belongings belonged to Jibraan.

Jibraan brought his parents to Rohi's home to see me. It was evening. I had just finished with my Maghreb prayer. Jibraan came to my room to inform me that he had come with his parents who were sitting with Rohi in her drawing room. I begged Jibraan for five minutes to join. In a great hurry, I rushed to the drawing room to meet them.

I was on cloud nine and my happiness knew no limits. I could see all the clouds, which kept on hovering over the horizon of my life, began to vanish away. I thanked Allah (God) for enabling me to exercise my personal discretion and choice in choosing a soul-mate for the first time. I was in a very jovial mood. I felt I was maturing as a complete woman. I was attaining freedom to take decisions for myself. My face had become the index of my happiness. This state of jubilance was quite a new feeling generated in my inner world where only sorrows, bondages and limitations had flourished. My emancipation from the bondages of man-made systems, which, too, were facilitated equally by a man – Jibraan– and a woman – Rohi, infused a great degree of confidence in myself and trust in my destiny that all the banes in my life were over after all.

Having all these feelings inside myself, I inched towards meeting an old couple who were eager to see me, not judge me, as this had already been done by their most capable son – Jibraan. Completely overtaken by the awe and aura of Jibraan's family, I moved towards the drawing room very slowly because my own internal fears about my misfortune were haunting me. I was continuously praying to Allah (God) that everything should pass conveniently and they may consent to our decision to marry.

Ultimately, I was on the door and stopped a step away when I heard Jibraan's father saying to him, 'Where is our would-be daughter-in-law? We are oldies and can't afford much waiting.' Before my absence could cause any discomfort and unease, I knocked and entered. When all their sights fell on me, Jibraan said: 'Here she is.' First Jibraan's mom, wearing a decent Pakistani fabric suit of white and pink and eyesight glasses hugged me and said: 'Jibraan, she is taller and more dashing than you are.' After I met his mom, his dad also stood and put his hand on my head, saying: 'God bless you.' Jibraan's dad was very graceful, tall, well dressed and very crisp in his talk. I sat near his mom who held my hand.

Jibraan's father told him with full confidence and with a dazzling blaze of feeling, 'Jibraan you are really a man with meticulous choice and now I can understand why you kept us waiting for your marriage. You are a gem, Jibraan, and you ultimately found your equal jewel. I was not expecting you to make such a drop-dead choice. And all our votes go in favour of our would-be daughter-in-law, Hoor, who is really an enchanting lady.'

Almost in a similar tone and spark of felicity, Jibraan's mom voiced very rhetorically, 'I don't understand anything, I don't know anything, I will not listen to anything at all but I want to take my daughter to our home right now.' Jibraan cross-conversed, 'Mom, please relax. We will take her properly within the next week or so.' Dad intervened, 'This is also our daughter's house and it is only a matter of few days and we will get her to her own house.'

Jibraan fixed Friday for our marital ceremonies and *Nikah*. All agreed including Rohi as most of the things had already been finalized by me with Jibraan and Rohi.

# Chapter Thirty

Meeting with Jibraan's family eliminated my feelings of impuissance. I had hardly nurtured any feelings of a daughter as my own father threw me into the dustbin of traditions and taboos by getting me married very early before puberty, and by not giving me any love of a daughter.

So, I had more experience of being a wife and a mother than a daughter and than a beloved. I was born anew in the family of Jibraan. I felt perfumed with the odour of my struggle, which stood retuned with my strong sense of achievements.

My power of being a woman was recharged, refurbished and regenerated. All my powers – the power of woman, the power of love, the power of intellect, the power of emotions, the power of daughter, the power of wife and also the power of mother got redefined and re-outlined in uniting with Jibraan, a real source of inspiration, motivation, and also correction in all terms.

Everything was going perfectly well. New developments in our relations chorded befittingly with our future roadmap.

A bolt from the blue came. Jibraan called me and shared some very heart-sinking news with me. He told me that some banned outfits were issuing threats to him for his being a liberal thinker on many counts, which the outlaws had allegedly underlined. Jibraan was an iron rod not to be melted with the heat of threats, so issued, but for us, as a family, it was a source of grave concern. More importantly, Jibraan shared this only with me, not even with his family or Rohi. He strictly forbade me to leak this to anyone because this would create panic in the family and friend circles.

This news created ripples of fear in us during our good days. The bubbles of terror were enlarging day by day and we were off our rockers. Being totally in a befuddled state of mind to deal with this tar baby, all our plans for happiness went haywire. After going through the mill, I again came across a problem that made my heart sink into sorrow. When the tough got going, the going got easiest.

Jibraan tried to hold his balances and nerves in a serious pickle. But he needed something more to brave the threat. I suggested him to discuss the matter with some seasoned police officers and go for some protection before it was too late to repent. At least, what we can do at our end, we must do without any delay.

On this Jibraan's response was very pessimistic and disappointing, as he had no trust in the police or agencies to save him from this kind of danger. He was of the strong view that since agencies and police are themselves falling daily victims to terrorist attacks and have lost a lot of good guys in this war against darkness so he could hardly see any light at the end of tunnel.

Therefore, whatever will be done, it will purely be done on the basis of self-help. For that he met with a retired senior police officer, who was a very good family friend of his father. According to Jibraan, his retired uncle had a very good understanding with him and would not disclose anything to his family.

The next day, early in the morning, Jibraan came to meet me to give final shape to the plan of marriage and threat avoidance. With a sinking heart and a very fallen face, he said: 'The war of truth is very difficult to wage. Ideals always tax and demand sacrifice.'

Jibraan spotlighted the fault-lines of the system. 'We live with humans in a society which has some of its own ideals to survive and thrive. Those ideals are not set by people like us but by those who control resources and those who matter in the power structure, which is yet to be dented and destroyed by the people of pen. The pen's power is yet to take roots in a society where gun power and muscle power reign supreme.

'I am intoxicated with the power of ideas and I have to face the madness of the lunatic fringe, who are overwhelmed by the power of violence. But I will have to face this; though I am alone today, tomorrow I will be joined by many, if I survive sometime to make my voice touch the hearts of general public here and abroad.'

Jibraan further expressed his longing for immediate marriage with these words: "I do not at all fear death, which I, like all other humans, have to face and taste. What am I really concerned about is, I don't want to die without marrying you. Our marriage will accomplish my mission. But another issue with me right at the moment is what to tell my parents as to why I am not going for formal arrangements; after all, I am their only son. So they crave to see my marriage celebrations.'

I requested Jibraan: 'I think the matter of threats by some terrorist networks which are very strong to carry out any attack anywhere in our country as is evident from the last few years in our chequered history of public peace should not be taken lightly and should not be dealt with individually without taking family on board. Though a very sore thing to share with family, at least their emotional support in times of tension and their prayers to God for keeping you safe do have some part to play, much better than you going and getting a guard and gun.'

Jibraan revealed something more serious: he had received a letter and messages on social media for getting ready to die. I asked Jibraan: 'Why don't you do something to get rid of all this rubbish?' He said, 'I have not yet responded to them because they did not give any other option to negotiate with them or strike some bargain therein.'

There was a twelve-word message which read:

'Mr Jibraan get ready to die, you have made enough mockery of our values.'

I asked Jibraan to engage them with some constructive response so that they would delay his execution, if so planned.

On my insistence, Jibraan shared with his parents who gave him really very good suggestions and who agreed to keep the marriage simple, closed, secret, and very low profile so that the attackers may not utilize this moment.

His father and his retired police uncle planned for him. Further they got my passport ready after preparation of *Nikah* papers in advance of marriage. They got a Visa for the UAE (United Arab Emirates) for us initially as it was easily done online. We were to move very clandestinely to Dubai on the very next day of our marriage.

# Chapter Thirty-One

Jibraan was not content with this cat-and-mouse game. But he had no other option to dodge the terrorist bullet. These days were very tough for me and for Jibraan's family as the terrorists had sent Jibraan pictures of his home and his father on the one hand while on the other we were preparing for *Nikah*.

Mr. Zamran Khan, the father of Jibraan Khan, consulted this problem of the threats issued to his son by some fanatics having objections to Jibraan's opinions and points of view on the system. Some old buddies of Jibraan's father from the army and the police service advised him four things to be followed religiously to save Jibraan's life; they were:

a. To take threats seriously;
b. Get Jibraan married expeditiously and very clandestinely;
c. Soon after *Nikah*, or marriage, send the couple abroad by making classified arrangements for their going abroad;
d. Restrict Jibraan's movements and tell him to engage the lunatics in negotiations to buy time.

Keeping in mind the advice of the veteran uncles, Jibraan responded to those who were posting him threats of dire consequences. Jibraan realized that their constant intimations meant that they were interested in something other than killing Jibraan instantly. Had it been so, they would have done so without much threatening stuff. This made sense to all of us.

Jibraan responded sending this message to one of the WebPages: 'Can we talk; is there any condition under which you could spare me?'

A reply came in two hours. They said: 'We will think about it under certain conditions!' His police uncle said on reading their message: 'They need something from you. They don't need your life. But they need something that is very special to you.'

Our curiosity was raised on the comments of police uncle. The scoundrels underlined certain conditions. But Jibraan and all of us were of the view that they would demand some money but the police uncle disagreed with us on ransom or extortion. However, we told Jibraan to ask them for conditions.

Jibraan did it writing to them: 'Ok, I will do my best to meet your conditions.' They quickly responded him: 'Think before you agree to comply with our demand, because once you agree you have to comply. And you have complete rights to decide between accepting and rejecting to do what we want you to do.'

Jibraan replied them: 'I am quite clear and I want to know your demand. Do you need some money?' This infuriated them and they wrote: 'Dear, don't insult us, we have plenty of riches and money. Either join our cause or get ready for consequences.' Jibraan was confused and asked them again as to what they wanted, and they wrote: 'Choose between death and allegiance to our cause.'

This bombshell stupefied Jibraan for a while but he succeeded in composing himself by intelligently asking them for some time. He asked them, 'Can you spare some time to let me choose between the options?'

They agreed but warned him not to play smart with them. They gave him two weeks to ponder and decide. They gave Jibraan an ultimatum, 'We can give you two weeks to decide and strictly warn you not to play smart with us. If anything goes wrong, it will go wrong at your own peril.'

We had only ten days sharp to make or to break as both the options either to join a terrorist network for any reason or to leave the world were not at all acceptable to any of us who enveloped Jibraan's life or who meant something to Jibraan himself as well. Therefore we decided to think of something in between.

Jibraan was of the strong view that 'joining a terrorist network is tantamount to leaving the world as well as leaving humanity; so I would prefer leaving the world as a human being instead of leaving humanity as a human locust by joining hands of extremists who have their own world view and their own notions of right and wrong that hardly fit well in the scheme of the conscience of a person like me.'

So, we decided to leave Pakistan on the wedding night. Everything at our end was completely ready: passports, visa, money etc. Interestingly, to our utter surprise we were lost in reverie that soon things would get back to normalcy and we would be back to Clifton Karachi very soon. Unfortunately, days of dismay and melancholy knew no ending since then.

We were unaware that someone very close to us was keeping a close eye on our activities. However, good thing in all episode was the advice of the police uncle who had strictly told us to keep our visa and passport things top secret and never to talk about anything related to the threats or anything like that in front of servants and other friends. We kept it to ourselves. Jibraan had confirmed our flight on our wedding night at 3am for Dubai. We formally wedded on a Friday night in April 2016 and after our initial ceremonies of *Nikah* were over at Jibraan's home, we had a tea with mom and dad who took us straight to Jinnah Airport where we reached safely at 2am and bade farewell to mom, dad and also my daughter and son who too accompanied us and who were to shift to Jibraan's house with his mom and dad.

Zuhra, my daughter, kept on crying as she had never lived without me but since her brother, who had joined the police as a constable, was with her, in addition to Jibraan's mom and dad, I was leaving feeling confident. My son, also moved by the moment, which he had not experienced before, could not stop shedding tears.

Jibraan's father and mother held his hands and their body language was quite reluctant to accept our departure. But for the sake of surviving a deathly crisis of life, we were left with no other option except to have the poison of departure. Our family advised us that it was better to leave the country than to leave the world for nothing.

The system, the very cruel system, the extremely hostile system, the system whose bases lay entangled in bondage, slavery, restriction, imprisonments, limitations and sanctions seeking to deny freedom of all kinds, including freedom of choice, freedom of thought, freedom of movement, freedom of associations, freedom of assembly, freedom of expression and freedoms of all kinds. The system badly lacked the safety and liberty mechanism for all and sundry on equal basis.

If there were some people who enjoyed freedom, they were the criminals; they were the outlaws; they were the influential; they were the people who had bullets and guns; that had control on libel. It presented the true picture of the Hobbesian state of nature where people were nasty, brutish and ruthless.

While we got onboard, Jibraan told me: 'You really don't know what I am feeling right at this moment. I am quite at the crossfire of happiness and grief. I am entangled in the claw of serious moral dilemma. Today is a very important day for me anyway. On the one hand, I have united with you forever and on the other, I am leaving my homeland, perhaps forever.'

Jibraan further reflected, 'It may be the first time for you to travel abroad but I have travelled many times. However, this time it is quite different for me. Anyway, it would definitely be a bizarre journey for both of us to be remembered for all the times to come.' On this, I told him, 'I am not very disappointed and believe this phase is, indeed, a difficult one but it will pass too as I have experienced much harder days before.'

But my continuous inner destruction knew no abating. Itching of heart and pricking of conscience regarding our so-called sensible act of leaving our homeland due to the fear of being killed by some anarchist forces. There was a very valid question knocking sense into my mind, 'Why should we bid farewell to our homeland? Who will mend the system and society we had grown up in?' To me, our escaping from our country appeared an act of cowardice and no substitute for our freedom! It was better to die while fighting than to retreat.

I could not control the feeling, while sitting on the plane which was one hour late due to a weather problem in Karachi, in asking Jibraan: 'Don't you think we are cowards, who are leaving their homeland to escape death which could catch us anywhere anytime, even on this plane? Do we presume that a miracle will happen in our country and angels will descend from above to bring our country back on track? Should we trust the torch-bearer of violence, crime, and extremism to bring some promising change for our offspring back home? Was it enough that we were born, grew up and enjoyed our home and when danger knocked at our country we thought it expedient to escape instead of doing something significant at any cost? Were our claims for patriotism hollow within and reflection of mere nostalgia, lacking meaning? Are we doing something noble like people of meaning do while being in a similar situation? Do we think we have any spark of decency?'

I further scolded Jibraan, 'In my scheme of personal point of view, the answers to all these questions run counter to what we should have done. I think we still have the option not to rethink but to leave the plane with keenness and motivation to keep on doing our best to make some difference at home while living with our own people, irrespective of threats, dangers, and challenges. I would love to live in my country, die for it, and die in it. My problem is with my system, not with my homeland, nor yet with my destiny. Man has been the bane of my life and man would remain the source of the solution of my problems.'

Finally, I played the tunes of my heart, which sounded nothing other than 'patriotism' or a call from deep inside for expressing the unfettered love for my soil. I took the riskiest decision of my life purely on the basis of my own inner convictions. On this, I very rhetorically told Jibraan: 'I am not going to leave my country at any cost. Be my true man and let us leave the plane before it leaves my soil whose fragrance I would feel nowhere but here in my country only.'

Jibraan was deeply moved and we stormed to leave the plane for home with a resolve to face whatever comes in our way at whatsoever sacrifice it demands. We promised each other that however murky our future may appear, nothing would stop us telling to the world what we think is true and what we believe is right. This was the mission and the riskiest decision ever; we had to live with it for the rest of our lives.